in praise of lies

BY THE SAME AUTHOR

THE KILLER

in praise of lies

PATRICIA MELO

Translated by Clifford E. Landers

BLOOMSBURY

Published by Bloomsbury Publishing, New York and London
Distributed to the trade by St. Martin's Press

A CIP catalogue record for this book
is available from the Library of Congress

ISBN 1-58234-058-7

First published in Brasil as *Elogio da mentira*
by Companhia das Letras, 1998

This edition first published in Great Britain 1999 by
Bloomsbury Publishing Plc

First U.S. Edition 1999
10 9 8 7 6 5 4 3 2 1

Typeset by Hewer Text Ltd, Scotland
Printed in the United States of America by
R.R. Donnelley & Sons Company,
Harrisonburg, Virginia

1

I've always liked snakes, especially the poisonous varieties, but it was because of Melissa that I began frequenting the Municipal Serological Institute. When we were introduced, she was standing in front of the museum's artificial lake – pretty, in a white lab coat and glasses, examining a ten-foot-long boa constrictor. We shook hands. 'You'll like what I'm about to do,' she said.

One of Melissa's assistants immobilized the snake by grasping it with both hands just below the head. Next the snake was placed on the laboratory table. 'She doesn't want to eat,' Melissa said, 'it's the stress of captivity. Look, the poor thing has fleas.' Another assistant brought a rabbit in a small cage. With his help, using a pair of tongs as a lever, Melissa pried open the reptile's mouth. Then she took the rabbit from the cage and, in a quick move, broke its neck. 'I always kill the prey before force-feeding,' Melissa said, introducing the dead rabbit into the boa's throat. 'Ophidians don't eat dead animals,' she said, 'but the prey's blood is still warm, so that's not a problem.' With her hands, Melissa squeezed the serpent's body, causing the rabbit to descend into the ophidian's stomach. 'You can take it away,' she told the assistant.

'Come on,' Melissa said. 'I'll show you the Institute. In the old days, this entire area was a forest reserve. Did you see the number of frangipani there are out there? In blossom time, everything around here has a wonderful smell.' We walked through the museum side by side, leisurely, and there was already something between us, threads, with her guiding the conversation and me observing the serpents in their vivariums. Melissa showed me her favorite, the desert viper, *Echis carinatus.* 'When it comes to killing,' she said, 'there's nothing better. Ninety per cent of those bitten die, even if they get the serum.'

We left the museum. The day was overcast, the sky dark. 'I like this place,' Melissa said. 'Look at these trees; that one there is over a hundred years old. Isn't it beautiful? What snake is the murderer going to use?'

'I haven't decided,' I said. 'I know there are many varieties of toxins.'

'Yes, you can take your pick. There are necrotizing venoms, neurotoxic venoms, which paralyze the muscles. What is it you're looking for?'

I explained that I was in the initial phase of research for the book and that I didn't know yet, but the idea of death by asphyxiation appealed to me.

'It's a terrible way to die,' she said. 'Some species of the genus *Naja* would be perfect. The problem is they don't exist in the Americas. If you want to use venom with neurotoxin, I suggest the corals. But you should know that accidents with coral snakes aren't very frequent; corals are timid and flee from man. That might cramp your story. We have to think about the place where the crime will be committed. Who are your victims?'

'Like I said,' I replied, 'I'm just beginning.'

Thunder rumbled across the sky, then lightning. We

didn't even have two minutes to dash back to the museum before the rain came pouring down.

Melissa got me a towel and I dried off. 'You're going to catch cold in that wet shirt; I'll get you a coat.'

'No,' I said.

'You're going to catch a cold,' she insisted. She went to a closet, took out a large yellowed lab coat. 'Put it on,' she said. 'It belonged to a biologist who died last year, do you mind?' I didn't mind. I went into the bathroom, took off my soaked shirt, and put on the coat, which smelled of mothballs. 'Fine,' Melissa said when I returned. 'Would you like to see the mice?'

While we waited for the rain to stop, she showed me the area where the mice were raised. A room full of cages with pups smaller than my thumb. 'From their mother's dug to the mouths of serpents,' Melissa said. 'Every two weeks I toss a handful of them into the serpentarium.'

Before I left, she invited me to attend the talk she was giving the next day to personnel from public-health clinics in the interior of the state. 'It's very technical and didactic,' she said. 'It might help you with your book.'

I accepted. That was how we began.

2

To: Wilmer From: José Guber
The Turk, or *He Buried His Mother and Went Swimming*, by Richard Higgins
John Sayers, a good, simple and eccentric fellow, loses his mother and does not cry at the wake. (And he even drinks the coffee with cream that the caretaker at the chapel offers him.) A few days later he kills a Turk on the beach, for no reason. He is tried and convicted, not for having killed the Turk but for not having cried at his mother's wake. Wilmer, the story seems simple but it's quite complex. It has some very interesting details: the prosecution bases its entire case on the fact that John Sayers didn't cry at his mother's wake, to which he came with his hair wet. We'll do a gripping detective story that will show how absurd our judicial system is. Please give your quick OK.

From: Wilmer To: José Guber
You are forbidden to write novels about eccentric weirdos who kill Turks on the beach for no reason. Haven't you read Memo 149? We don't kill Turks, blacks, Jews, Indians, children, maids, endangered animal species and the like. I also forbid you to write about any theme dealing with our judicial system. I want a different outline.

Four months earlier, I was on the Internet researching African snakes, thinking about copying the plot of *The Adventure of the Speckled Band* for the Spitting Fire series, even though I found the story kind of boring, when I found a home page that interested me. It was Melissa's. 'I am a member of the São Paulo Association of Herpetology,' she said, 'and work at the Municipal Serological Institute. I have a collection that includes a true boa and a reticulated python. If you are interested in these animals, have questions, or desire information, please get in touch with me.'

I felt attracted by her photo, showing a serpent wrapped around her arm and a book in her right hand. Anyone with a book in their hand is always a hope. Short, straight hair, thick eyebrows – I liked her. I sent a message asking for information about venoms. I explained I was a writer of detective novels who was writing a story in which the murderer used serpents as the weapon for his crimes. Melissa answered the same day, saying that the first thing she read in the papers was the police reports and that she could help me with information about snake venom, toxins, and poisoning in general. We made an appointment for the next day at the serpentarium in the Institute.

That night, at home, I was excited. I started reading two books, gave up on both in the first few pages, sat down, got up, turned on the TV, went to the living room, returned to the bedroom, rummaged through the bookshelves, sat down, ate ten apples, got up, took a hot shower, twenty minutes under the shower. Only then was I able to read. It wasn't easy to write my outlines. Sometimes it was necessary to read three or four books to find something. I enjoyed that, not writing – I never liked writing – I liked to lie in bed reading, drifting off and waking up minutes later, going back to my reading, I would read a little and sleep, sometimes I would dream about passages from stories, wake up, read a bit more, eat, sleep, the whole night like that, reading and sleeping, and eating chocolate, mixing it all together in my head, sometimes I would also note something down on the computer, that's how I worked.

Midnight. I warmed a cup of milk in the kitchen, got the medicine, and went to my mother's room. She was on her knees, head bowed, praying. Images of saints covered the walls. My mother hadn't been out of the house for more than two years, since Moisés, my older brother, died of leukemia. She asked if I had closed all the windows, locked the door, turned off the gas. She asked if I could buy her a megaphone. 'What do you want with a megaphone?' I asked. It was to put next to the picture of Our Lord Jesus Christ, she explained. It had to be a really powerful one; she wouldn't place a cheap megaphone beside Jesus Christ. I promised her I'd buy one. I pulled the blanket over my mother and kissed her. As I was leaving her room, she asked me if I was keeping my promise not to stay up all night reading. I said I was.

'That's nice, son,' she said. 'Those books were ruining you.'

3

Urutus, jararacas, cascavéis, jararacuçus, surucutingas, cotiaras – I saw these and many other serpents in the slides that Melissa projected during her talk. I also saw pictures of a dog paralyzed by a rattlesnake bite, mummified feet from an accident with *jararacas*, and many, many victims of accidents with snakes, some without an arm, others missing a foot, a leg – quite a show.

The auditorium at the Institute was empty. Besides me there were only seven hicks, employees of public-health stations in the interior, who needed basic lessons in applying antivenin. I made myself comfortable in the first row, right beside the screen, fixed my gaze on Melissa and didn't let up for a minute. A healthy-looking young woman, a snake nutritionist. She was wearing a tight blue dress that showed her shape well. Now and then I heard a few words, some phrase about the efficacy of the various antitoxic substances, the applying of serums. 'Disinfect the area with alcohol,' she said, 'use disposable needles,' but I wasn't paying attention to the words, I wasn't there to listen, I wanted to look, wanted to see and I did see, saw muscular arms, nape, neck, saw small hands, unpainted nails, just the way I liked them. And white teeth. Muscles. 'Stop that,' she said, when she passed by me. I didn't stop. I went on looking. 'Fresh,' she said, but I know she liked it. In fact, she told me later, 'I liked it. You looked like a butcher,' she said.

That night, while we had dinner, Melissa complimented my idea of using snakes as the weapon for my crime. She already had a plan sketched out in her mind; I was part of that scheme and suspected nothing. 'You've created a very intelligent crime,' she said.

'I haven't created anything yet,' I said. 'I'm going to create it.' But she didn't hear me.

'How can the police prove it wasn't an accident?' she said. 'Think along with me: the woman takes her husband to a hotel in the country, far from hospitals and public-health clinics –'

'More wine?' I asked.

'Yes,' she replied. 'If the woman,' she continued, 'if the woman works in a serological center like me, she'll know the clinics that don't have antivenins and choose a hotel in that area. Think about it, it'll be easy to arrange a *Bothrops jararaca*; a lot of dealers show up at the institutes trying to sell snakes illegally. You saw the statistics I showed; *Bothrops jararaca* is responsible for 88 per cent of the recorded accidents in the country, and they're everywhere. Think of it. The murderer can also use a *Bothrops alternatus,* which as the country folk say either kills or cripples. It's easy to take a snake as part of your luggage, in the trunk of the car. It's easy to get the husband drunk. It's easy to make the snake bite him while he's sleeping with his belly full like a disgusting pig. And it's easy to claim it was an accident.'

'I'm not planning to write a crime of passion,' I said.

'Who are you going to kill?' she asked.

'Two heiresses,' I replied.

'I thought it was a couple,' she said. 'Anyway, it applies to anyone. The important thing is the logistical set-up. If she works in a serpentarium and her husband dies from a snake-bite, the police are going to say to themselves, "The woman wouldn't be so stupid as to do that." It's so obvious that it's no longer suspicious. Am I wrong? There's even a film like it, with that blonde woman, I forget her name. Do you think the police would suspect me, if I killed my husband like that?'

That's how I found out that Melissa was married.

'The interesting thing about this story,' she said, 'besides the fact of it being a scientific murder, is the symbolic aspect. In some cultures, snakes represent life, light, immortality. The Egyptians, the Hindus, and the Australian Aborigines venerate serpents. You can't kill snakes in certain parts of Africa. It's a very serious crime. But for us, the serpent is merely the symbol of malediction, lies, and cruelty. Do you remember the anathema that God cast upon the serpent? "Thou art cursed above every beast of the field; upon thy belly shalt thou go, and dust shalt thou eat all the days of thy life. Thou shalt be pursued and slain without mercy and nothing canst thou do to redeem thyself." I must have been seven the first time I heard that passage from the Bible; it was in catechism class. I thought God was an idiot to expel from paradise an animal as superior as the serpent. There's nothing more interesting than snakes, nothing, absolutely nothing. Any animal – giraffe, zebra, elephant – biologically speaking, all those mammals are nothing compared to a serpent. I've always loved ophidians.'

At that moment in the conversation, we were facing each other across the table, drinking wine, each looking at the other, laughing at any piece of foolishness, Melissa's hands in mine, but she still wasn't completely relaxed; she was still holding back. I would insist, interlace our fingers, she would withdraw her hand. It took some time for her to feel at ease, and when that happened, I said, 'Let's go to my place.'

I took Melissa to my messy room, papers everywhere, piles and piles of books spread on the floor. I showed her the books I had published with Minnesota and which were sold at newsstands under American pseudonyms: *When the Sun Hides Its Face,* by Gregory Turow; *The Seven Monks,* by John Condon; *The Statue's Curse,* by Malcolm Lovesey, and many others. 'Why pseudonyms?' she wanted to know.

'It's a requirement of the publisher,' I said. She thought that José Guber was a very artistic name. I explained that my publisher wasn't artistic.

'You must be very creative to dream up all those crimes, to think of weapons, alibis, escapes – it must not be easy.' Very difficult, I agreed. 'I'd like to read some. May I take them?'

That night nothing happened. Nor the next. We stayed in my room talking about snakes and crime the whole time. 'I'm going to confess something to you,' she said. 'I like to read about crime. I haven't the time for fiction, I only read scientific texts about the effects of snake venom, but crime, I like to read about crimes in the papers, not common crimes, I like it when I see a human being explode, someone killing his entire family, or else just the opposite, very elaborate crimes, a work of art, an artist, a well-planned crime is a work of art, don't you agree?'

The third time we met, it happened. She was reading something, I don't know what, I didn't pay attention, I yanked the book from her hand and approached. Kisses, I pulled her with my body toward the bed. She said I could believe it or not, but she'd never done that before, that it was the first time she'd ever betrayed her husband. She didn't used the word betray, or husband; she spoke in a different way, she was courageous, she was aggressive, and gentle, she pulled me by the hair, 'Come,' she said.

4

To: Wilmer From: José Guber

The Black Angora, by Hillary McClure

Disappeared: Nora Waugh, thirty-three, wife of the multi-millionaire industrialist Thomas Waugh. The detective Scott Condon takes the case. The search begins. Everything leads him to believe that Nora ran away with her lover. (Important detail: with her, Nora took her Angora cat, which she was crazy about, according to the servants. Attention: the husband hated the cat and constantly mistreated it, once even putting out one of its eyes.) The case is filed away. At the end, a surprising scene. The industrialist Thomas Waugh invites the investigator Scott to see his wine cellar. (He's very unhappy because his wife deserted him and he wants to tie one on with the detective.) Scott, the detective, agrees. In the cellar, Thomas starts spouting a lot of nonsense such as 'These walls are very solid.' He taps on the wall with his cane: 'See how solid the walls are?' Then Scott hears something that sounds like the weeping of a child, a frightening cry, coming from behind the walls. He calls a support team and tears down the cellar wall. Nora Waugh's body is there, buried in the wall, beside a small black Angora cat, which is meowing from hunger. The husband confesses the crime.

From: Wilmer To: José Guber

OK. Outline approved. But let's change the black cat to a black parrot. The millionaire, one of those eccentric fucks, paints the parrot black just to irritate his wife. Another thing, in the final scene, Scott doesn't hear a cry, he hears the parrot saying, 'She's here, she's here!' The rest stays the same. Wilmer.

P.S. I changed my mind. I'm going to ask Calisto to make some adaptations and use this outline for the Monsters of Terror series. Send me another outline this afternoon.

In the following days, I was overcome by a feeling of well-being; everything seemed to be going well, and I felt calm, happy, enthused. Every morning Melissa would come to my apartment, we would get between the sheets, we loved each other, everything was enjoyable, she read all my books, actually read them, with tremendous rigor, commenting, making suggestions, and that was very good, very good and very useless, since I could no longer rewrite them or wanted to. Melissa wasn't interested in bloody psychopaths. She hated crafty, wisecracking detectives. Her preference was for homicide where victim and murderer knew each other, crimes of passion, treacherous partners; she also liked poisons and diabolical women who seduced and corrupted weak men. She loved to discuss the perfect crime, whether it was one committed without premeditation, a crime of opportunity as the specialists call it, or one thoroughly planned. She read *A Train to Death*, by Martin Clark, several times. 'Your books ought to be sold in bookstores,' she said, 'instead of newsstands, and they ought to be better printed.' It didn't matter to me if they were sold at newsstands.

At that time, I should state, I wrote books, but I wasn't a

writer, I was a kind of worker in the canning section of a sausage factory. We had a deadline to deliver the books, the sausages – two weeks, and not even one day beyond that. I wasn't uncomfortable stealing stories from the classics, not really, because I felt I was doing people a favor by giving the less fortunate reader the chance to read Shakespeare, Chesterton, Poe, and many other important authors. I had once stood at a newsstand observing who my readers were. People of all types, guys with the faces of office boys, a sad woman with the face of a housewife, nervous women who looked like manicurists, brokers of something or other carrying black briefcases. People who would never read the classics. I was doing them a favor; that was the truth.

In short, everything was going well.

On my birthday, Melissa came to the apartment carrying a red package, large and with gold ribbons. I opened it. Inside, curled up, a four-foot-long boa constrictor with yellow coloration and two sets of circular black marks on its back. 'She likes to eat cavies,' Melissa said.

I didn't want to accept it. 'No way,' I said. 'Take this animal back.'

'No,' she said, 'she's only going to eat cavies when she's an adult, and you can substitute rabbits for the cavies if you like, or several mice.'

'No,' I said.

'Lots of people raise snakes. I do, the Europeans do, in the United States it's sweeping the country. I'll help you set up the pen.'

'I think it's better I don't. My mother must be afraid of snakes.'

'Your mother never comes in here,' Melissa said. 'She doesn't leave her room. I've been your girlfriend for three months and I've seen her exactly twice. All she does is pray, the poor thing. We'll put a curtain over the bookcase, and when your mother comes in we'll lower it.'

Melissa had me buy litter, pens for shelter and feeding, warming pads, saucers, a hook to hang the snake on, everything. We emptied out two shelves of the bookcase and I set up the tanks. After a few days, I was already beginning to like it.

One interesting thing about raising snakes, unlike what happens with all other animals, is that there's not that mushy relationship, that sick need that cats have to be petted or that adoration that dogs feel for their owners. That's an advantage. And another good thing is the habit of contemplation. We don't contemplate rabbits, birds, or cats; only snakes attract us in this way, obliging us to look at and admire them. The serpent's diabolical charisma and its fearful beauty have an extraordinary power over us. Sometimes I would be at the computer writing my stories and I would get hooked. Come here, she, the boa, would order. Her bifid tongue. Admire my eyes. I would stand in front of the pen, hypnotized. Admire. Large, lidless eyes. Admire.

I still remember the first time I picked her up. I felt the cool touch of her skin sliding over my arm. She curled around my neck, slithered down my back. 'That's right,' Melissa said. 'Let her get used to you.' And then she defecated on me. 'That's normal,' Melissa explained, 'she's alert.'

I really came to like it. As I said, Melissa had a mid-size collection, with rare species acquired from smugglers who would show up at the Institute. She spent two hours a day taking care of the serpents, feeding, hygiene, that sort of thing, and she also talked to them, to the snakes. 'Not that I like talking with snakes,' she said, 'but at my house it's better to talk to snakes than – well, let's change the subject.'

Once, Melissa suggested we take our snakes for a walk in some park. She picked me up at home, in her car, very early, before 7 a.m., and we went to the university campus, me and my boa, Melissa and her albino Burmese python. We let the pair loose on the grass and stood there holding hands, kissing and watching our snakes warm themselves in the sun. We repeated the outing several times, until one day a female student athlete, some imbecile out jogging, saw our ophidians and ran screaming across the campus, the idiot. We had to hide our serpents quickly, and snakes are very sensitive, they get stressed over nothing. My boa went without eating for twenty days after the incident.

I never felt any fear of my boa, but in the first days when we slept together, my boa and I, I dreamed that she was wrapping herself around me from head to toe, slowly breaking all my bones with incredible strength. I awoke with the same sensation, paralyzed with fear and a cold liquid running over my body.

I commented on it to Melissa. 'Excellent,' she said, 'use that feeling of terror to describe your crimes and your characters. Put it to good use.'

5

From the beginning, I was in the driver's seat. The truth is that, in matters of love, there's no such thing as happenstance. We invent love. Of course, we have an instinctive sense of direction, our hormones are the arrow, we imagine the place where it can be hidden, love, and stick our hand in there to see what happens. Generally, there's a hole and nothing else. I found Melissa. She said she had especially liked my maniacal eyes, when we saw each other for the first time in the serpentarium. 'It was as if your gaze entered my flesh,' she said, 'pierced my flesh. You seemed like a butcher, a merchant, a horse trader.' She also said that I possessed strength, virility, and that I walked like a monkey, and that appealed to her from the start. Women love men who walk like monkeys. 'Even before you chose me,' she said, 'I had already chosen you.' That same day she came to me with that story that made my hair stand on end. I had never thought about it. Absolutely never. It was Melissa who started it. She asked if I believed in my theory of the three fundamentals of the perfect crime. I didn't remember writing that. 'Want to hear?' she said. 'It's in your book *A Train to Death.*' She got it from the bookcase and began reading:

Are you thinking about drowning your husband in the swimming pool? Everything will be found out within forty-eight hours. That's the act of an amateur. Want to do it right? Rule number one: Have an accomplice. Everyone needs help, no one gets away with it without accomplices – unless, of course, you confess everything and claim self-defense. Rule number two: You, the murderess, have to be a well-informed woman, know everything about the victim, everything, absolutely everything. Rule number three: This is the golden one. Be audacious if you want to kill your husband. See how the pros do it. First, set up the show. The guy's girlfriend, this is important, is part of the gang of killers. At the end of the day, the girl phones the killers and gives them all the information, says that they're going to such-and-such movie theater, such-and-such showing, such-and-such time. So then, the couple arrives in the automobile. Europa Theater. There's a parking place across the street, and that's where the victim parks. The two get out of the car; he puts the keys in his pocket. And then, with everyone watching, there in front of everybody, the guys come up to him. The killers. Everyone there, watching, couples, the popcorn vendor, the ticket seller, all of them there, and they don't hesitate, the killers, they fire without mercy. The victim is riddled from top to bottom, twenty, thirty bullets. He falls. The guys run off; the scheme involves a getaway car and driver. Of course, all of them already have alibis set up. The police know who did it. They arrest everybody, slap everybody around, but there's such a thing as habeas corpus. They can't prove who the guilty parties are. So everything works out fine, with impunity.

Melissa asked me if that was true, if there was an effective way of killing a person and staying out of the hands of the police. I replied that in Brazil it was even easier, that she could even drown her husband in the pool if she wanted to. 'I'm going to drown him,' she said. She said it just like that, without preamble, without explanation of any kind, nothing, one foot resting on her knee, her hand on her stomach, all very natural.

Melissa had never spoken ill of Ronald, which had in fact pleased me from the start. A woman loses 60 per cent of her charm when she begins to speak ill of her husband. Therefore, when she said she was going to drown Ronald, I didn't take the comment seriously. I ignored it, got up, turned on the computer. 'I'm going to do some work,' I said. I didn't give the matter any further thought.

All of that began at the first of the year. But it was only in June that she laid her cards on the table. This is precisely how it happened. My boa had escaped from its pen. I called Melissa and asked her to help me recapture it; it was the first time it had occurred. Melissa came to my apartment, we gave my mother a sleeping pill, waited for her to go to sleep, then spread supermarket bags in the hallway, bathroom, and living room. When the snake ran into the plastic it would make a noise and that way we'd be able to locate it. That was how you captured them; Melissa had read that somewhere. We turned out all the lights and sat on the sofa, holding hands, waiting for my serpent to make a move. Total silence; all I could hear was Melissa's breathing.

I put my hand on her knee. 'Take off your clothes,' I said.

'No,' she replied. 'Quiet, we have to find the serpent.'

'Take your clothes off,' I said, 'let's make love here on the sofa.'

'What about your mother?'

'She's asleep.'

'What about the boa?' she asked.

I moved closer, stuck my hand under her blouse, moved closer. She whispered in my ear, moaning, 'Have you had an idea how to kill Ronald?'

I stood up, turned on the lights. 'Turn out those lights,' she said, 'you're going to frighten the boa.' I didn't turn them out.

'He abuses me, he beats me.'

'Get a separation,' I said.

'I've tried nothing else for the last few years. He won't leave me alone; he threatens to kill me.'

'No,' I said. 'That's definite.'

'He knows,' she said, turning out the lights.

'Knows what?' I turned on the lights.

'About us. That we're lovers. Turn out that goddamn light.'

'Deny it,' I said.

'You don't understand. He doesn't suspect; he knows.'

'Lie, make something up, do something, but don't ask that of me.'

'Am I going to have to do it by myself? Is that what you're telling me? You're a man, you seduce me, I taught you everything, everything, all that I know about snakes, about poisons, toxins, you seduce me, you didn't know anything about toxins, about cruel ways of dying, I was the one who taught you, helped you, I gave you a snake,' she said, turning out the lights, 'a boa, and now you're telling me you're not going to kill my husband?'

'What are you saying?' I said, turning on the lights. 'One thing's got nothing to do with the other.'

'Yes, it does. You said you loved me and now you want out.'

'Helping to kill someone?' I said. 'Look what you're asking of me.'

'I'm asking you to help me to live. He's going to kill me if you don't kill him.'

'You never told me anything and now you want me to kill your husband.'

'I did tell you. I told you I was married.'

'Married, yes, but you never told me Ronald beat you.'

'What about the bruises?'

'What bruises?' I asked.

'You yourself were always asking me, "What are those bruises?" They were from the beatings. Are you telling me you never suspected?'

'Never.'

'Liar. You knew I was being beaten.'

'I didn't know any such thing.'

'And what about when I broke a tooth? What did you think?'

'I believed what you told me, a fall in the pool.'

'You're the only one who believed it. My dentist didn't swallow the lie.'

'That's enough,' I said.

'You seduce me, now you're abandoning me.'

'I'm not abandoning you, I'm saying that I'm not a murderer.'

'Coward,' she said, 'coward, I'll kill him myself, don't worry, I'll kill him for the two of us, stay here writing your little books, your little crimes, you coward, I'm going to kill him by myself.' And bang, she slammed the door, leaving me flat-footed in the living room.

In those days I was already nuts about Melissa. When we were in bed, I used to say, 'I enter your body and everything in me, my blood, my cells, my atoms, my electrons, screams, "I love this woman."' I didn't even remember the other women. Melissa came like a wave in an angry ocean, one of those you see on television, gigantic, covering everything. Except that I wasn't capable of killing anybody. It was one thing to write about fictitious crimes and another, completely different, to kill a human being, to pull the trigger, stick in the knife, strangle him, or whatever.

I awoke to the sound of a voice coming through a megaphone, getcher tangerines, they're large, they're sweet, they're juicy, getcher tangerines, our tangerines are tasty, four big boxes of tangerines, two bucks a box, getcher oranges, thin-skins, getcher oranges, sweet oranges, thin-skins. Then another voice, female, also through a megaphone, answered, getcher thick-skinned oranges, rotten oranges, getcher expensive oranges, our oranges are expensive, they're sour, they're Japanese, getcher sour tangerines, getcher fruit from hell.

I recognized the female voice: my mother's. I got out of bed, opened the blinds and saw the Japanese, in a van with a megaphone in his hand, sweet papaya, he was saying, rotten papaya, my mother replied, also with a megaphone in her hand, at the window next to mine. High-quality papaya, he was saying, rotten papaya from hell, my mother replied, sweet oranges, he said, oranges with maggots, rejoined my mother.

Some of the local residents, leaning on their windowsills, were watching the show, amused by my mother's behavior. I put on a shirt, went to the hall, knocked on her bedroom door. She ignored me, rotten papaya, she yelled, rotten Japanese papaya. I went back to the window. The neighbors were laughing. The vendor tried to come to an understanding, in his megaphonic voice, my friend, give me a break, he said. I'm not your friend, Japan-man, my mother replied.

The vendor put away his megaphone, got into his car, started the motor, and left. The neighbors were pleased. They applauded. 'Thank you, folks. Tomorrow it's the ice-cream man,' my mother said.

'Those street vendors drive me crazy,' she said when she opened the door to her room. 'If it's not ice-cream it's pots and pans, it's knife-sharpening, or grapes, I can't even pray.'

'Call the mayor's office if you want to lodge a complaint about street vendors,' I said.

'There's no way I'm going to call the mayor's office,' she said, 'I'm going to do what they do. I'm going to scream. It was God who gave me the idea. I was praying, and I couldn't concentrate because of some fruit vendor. God said to me: Buy a megaphone and do the same as he does,' my mother said, clutching the megaphone affectionately to her chest.

I took a shower, fixed my mother's breakfast. As I was leaving, I saw Melissa's panties on the sofa. I stuck them in my pocket and headed straight for the vivarium.

6

From: José Guber To: Wilmer da Silva
The Mirror, by Ed Mason
In keeping with your suggestion, I'm creating a simple narrative. I should add that I found your suggestion a very good one.

Imagine a fat priest with an innocent face who tells the following story, in the first person:

An actress was murdered. Three people saw the killing in the corridor of the theater leading to the dressing room. I was one of them. The corridor was a bit dark, so no one had a clear view of the scene. The investigations began. The judge called us to testify. The first witness said the following: I'm sure the killer was a woman. Something strange was coming from her head, maybe hair, if that can be called hair. The second witness stated that he didn't know if the killer was a woman or a man; the killer seemed more like a wild animal. The animal was husky and had a resemblance to an orang-utan. When the judge asked me if I had also seen the murderer, I answered in the affirmative. The man I saw was myself, I said. How so? asked the judge. There was a mirror at the end of the corridor, I said, close to where the woman's body was; therefore, the man I saw was myself, my own image reflected in the mirror. You mean, the judge said, that the first witness, who saw that animal with things coming out of its head, was describing herself? Yes, I said. You mean, the judge said, that the gentleman who saw the husky orang-utan was actually looking at himself in the mirror?

From: Wilmer da Silva To: José Guber
Even a child can see this story doesn't have the makings of a novel. There's no meat to it. You have just ten days to get a book to me.

'She didn't come to work today,' said the woman at the entrance to the vivarium.

The sun was shining outside, and I didn't know what to do with myself. All I could do was keep on squeezing Melissa's panties in my pocket and drinking coffee, one cup after another, coffee with artificial sweetener, eight espressos; I only stopped because my heart started racing. A blazing sun. I went to a pay phone and did something I hadn't dared do till that moment: I called Melissa's house. A man's voice answered. I hung up.

I loitered near the door to the Institute, not knowing what to do. I wanted to tell her that the first thing that comes into a woman's mind when she thinks about killing her husband is a fake robbery. The classic scene: she leaves the kitchen door unlocked, the murderer enters stealthily, goes to the living room, and the husband is dead before he even knows what's happening. The detectives show up and discover that the kitchen door wasn't jimmied, that on the night of the crime the children were sent to sleep at their grandmother's house, along with the dog, and it was the cook's night off. The way the police find the killer is also classic. On a raid in the slums, the police arrest a guy buying drugs. In his wallet is a check from the widow. Trial and conviction. That's what I was going to say to Melissa. I'll talk to your husband if you want me to. We'll hire a lawyer. You can move in with me till everything calms down. That's what I was going to say.

That was when the vivarium door opened and Melissa appeared in the garden. I noticed that her right arm was bandaged. With her other arm she was holding two cages of mice. She went into the serpentarium. The snakes, spread out on the ground or coiled around tree limbs, did not react to her presence. Melissa bent down, releasing the mice from the cages. Only then did she see me. I went over to her. She leaned against the wall of the serpentarium and asked if I had ever seen the snakes attack. 'It's pretty,' she said. I noticed a cut on her right eyebrow, and a purple bruise.

'How did that happen?' I asked. Melissa sighed, discouraged, and said that things were getting bad and that it was best we not see each other again.

'Turn around,' she said. 'Walk away. It's for the best.'

I didn't turn around. I didn't walk away. To tell the truth, it never even passed through my mind.

'Let's go to my place,' I said. 'You can't work with your arm like that.'

7

Wilmer, the publisher of the Spitting Fire series, sitting on the edge of his desk, was reading aloud to me another outline that I'd sent him the morning before. 'Listen up, Guber. I'm going to read this nonsense you wrote:

> We have here an old miser woman, senile and useless. If Igor, the poverty-stricken student, kills her, he can steal her money and do something useful for society. How to evaluate such behavior? Is it merely a crime? Igor, with the old woman's money, can study, become a philosopher, a thinker, be creative, revolutionize things. The old woman, as I said, is a useless piece of meat, an exploiter of the poor. What good is such a human being, after all? What need does society have of her? None, clearly. Will Igor kill the old woman? Yes, Igor will commit the crime. Igor will also kill the old woman's sister, another useless person, so that we have not one but two very bloody crimes. Igor gets away. And then his torture begins. Remorse and repentance. An intelligent policeman, Fyodor Negrev, predicts the moment when that conscience-stricken scrap of humanity will confess his crime.

'Frankly, do you find that interesting? The story takes place in Russia. I never heard of a Russian detective story. I don't even think they know what one is; there is no more Russia. Did you say Vilmer? You've been here almost two years and still don't know my name? My name is English, Wil-mer, with a w-sound. You don't say Vashington, you say Washington. The same thing with my name. My mother was English. To our readers, Russia ended with the fall of the Berlin Wall, and that's the truth. Who cares about guilt and repentance? We want action. Blood. Violence. You've written fourteen books and haven't learned that yet? Have you read Van Dine's rules? They're posted on the wall, Van Dine's rules. A detective story needs a dead body, and the more bodies it has, the better. And it can't be just any dead body. How are we going to arouse the spirit of revenge in readers by killing some mangy, undesirable old woman? When an old woman like that dies, people cheer. Another thing: a spectacular crime is one perpetrated by some pillar of the Church or the police, a nun, a professional benefactress, a governor. Van Dine said that, it's on the wall, all you have to do is read it, and you give me a killer who's a poor, idiotic student and Russian to boot? Just read Van Dine's rules. They're on the wall, golden rules, and the main one is this: detective stories need a detective, somebody who can put clues together and point out whodunit. If the reader already knows who killed the old woman, what do you need a detective for?'

I'd been thinking of asking Wilmer for an advance, but I had to leave quietly, with nothing. The moment wasn't right. Wilmer had been looking at me very strangely lately. Maybe he knew I was broke.

Wilmer's new secretary was in the corridor when I left. Nice legs. 'The guy's a total mulatto,' she said, 'and he goes around saying he's English. English my foot, he's mulatto. The guy has a black's yellow eyes and goes around claiming he's English. I never saw an English mulatto. I'm the one who's white with blue eyes, genuinely German. My name is Ingrid. You're Guber, I know. Would you like some coffee?'

I couldn't waste time. Melissa was waiting for me.

At six, we parked the car at the corner of the Colombina construction supply store, which occupied an entire block on Lutero Mendes. Six cash registers, two valets, and two security guards. According to Melissa, Colombina had two more stores in São Paulo, not as large as that one, but in any case Ronald was well off. 'I don't care at all about money,' she said, 'but it's a fact that we're going to come into a lot of money. We'll be able to put your mother in a nursing home. And if you want to, you can write your books and I'll publish them. Money won't be a problem.'

That offended me. There's nothing more irritating than people who keep rubbing the smell of money in your face, most of all when you need it. 'Sorry,' Melissa said, 'I was just trying to look on the bright side.'

'I don't want to put my mother in a nursing home,' I said.

'Of course not. We're not going to do that. It was just an idea.'

Chunky, nondescript, with fat feet, that's how I pictured him. I could close my eyes and see him in his tennis outfit, socks up to his knees, the racket on his shoulder. It wasn't hard to imagine his adipose belly. Successful businessmen always have a paunch; the paunch starts to grow when they give up fucking, or vice versa.

'See him? He's the one in the polo shirt,' Melissa said. Ronald was completely different from what I had thought. Tall, slim, elegant, a young husband with the eyes of a harmless dog. I couldn't check his feet to see whether they were extremely fat as Melissa had described them. But in any case, I would never say that a guy like him would batter women.

He got in his car and left. We sat there in silence, watching the activity in front of the store.

'We have to get a toad,' I said.

We didn't use the word *crime* in speaking of our plans. We spoke of 'doing the thing'. And the 'thing' was very simple. We would fake an accident with a poisonous snake at a hotel in the countryside, in the interior of São Paulo. The idea wasn't new; for some time Melissa had been planning every detail, but she liked to say she had gotten everything from my book *Serpents That Kill.* I hadn't written a book called *Serpents That Kill*; I hadn't even gone as far as submitting the outline. All I had done was tell Melissa, at the time when we were beginning our involvement, that I was thinking about doing a story in which the killer used snakes as his weapon. The rest she came up with on her own, including the title.

Later, in bed, after sex, Melissa showered me with praise, told me I was very good at it. 'Good at what?' I asked.

'At crimes,' she replied. 'You know how to set them up, you're concerned with details, consequences, alibis, weapons, everything. Why didn't I think of a toad? It's perfect, a toad. My father always used to say that if a toad comes into the house it's fleeing from a snake. Country hotels have toads and snakes. I defy any detective to say they don't. You promise you won't back out?' she asked.

'I promise.'

'Then say it.'

'I promise that I'm going to kill Ronald.'

'And that you won't cheat on me.'

'Never,' I said.

'Say: I promise I'm going to cut off his feet.'

'What?'

'I hate his feet,' she said. 'They're the part that disgusts me the most. His feet and his face. You told me you would cut off his feet.'

'I said that?' I asked.

'Yes, yesterday, in bed.'

It was true. I had said it.

8

From: José Guber To: Wilmer da Silva
Who Killed Larry Manson?, by Richard Carr
The multimillionaire Larry Manson dies mysteriously in his office. We have several suspects, the butler, relatives, heirs, upstairs maids, pantry maids, the doorman, etc. The intellectually gifted detective Dashiel Traver is called in to head the investigation. Questioning, searches, the usual activity. And then, the surprise. Who is the murderer – the butler? No. The heir? No. The murderer is simply the narrator himself, the medical doctor Roger Cain, a good friend of Larry Manson's, a citizen above suspicion, who even helps Dashiel Traver in the investigation.

Wilmer liked the outline a lot. I had finally gotten on the board. 'This business of the narrator being the killer is an innovative idea,' he'd said on the phone, the ignorant fool, 'and innovation, you know, is always our objective. I've even thought of some changes for the next few books,' he said.

'It would be great if we improved the covers,' I said.

'No,' he said, 'I'm keeping the covers. The public likes that combination of lipstick, revolver, and pools of blood. I'm thinking of putting a note about the author on the last page. The Americans do that. Let me read you the short bio I did for the author of *Who Killed Larry Manson?*. Listen: "Richard Carr was born in Chicago, and he and his parents moved to New York when he was seven. Part of his adolescence was spent in England, France, and Germany. Today he lives in Canada with his wife and their Chihuahua dog. His hobby is salmon fishing." What do you think?'

I started writing day and night, while Melissa checked the supply of snake antivenin at every health clinic in the rural areas of the São Paulo interior, work that had to be done at night, in the Institute's files.

Monday morning, Wilmer phoned to set up a meeting at the office.

'Read just the underlined part,' he said, handing me a Xerox copy as soon as I sat down in the chair across from his desk. 'Out loud.'

I read: '*Twenty Rules for Writing Detective Stories.* S. S. Van Dine. Rule number 4. The detective or any of his investigators should never be the guilty party. That constitutes outright cheating.'

I put down the sheet and looked at Wilmer. From the front, he was an ordinary guy. But when he turned around, a small caudal appendage, as if it were an appliqué, was visible at the back of his head, a small ponytail held by a rubber band like those used in banks to hold money. What statement was he trying to make with that little tail? And his with-it T-shirts? I'd always had nothing but disdain for that kind of youth-worshipper.

'In your story *Who Killed Larry Manson?*,' he said, 'the killer is the narrator, a highly regarded doctor, isn't that so? Don't you think it's the same thing?' I replied that the narrator is the narrator, not the detective.

'Yes,' he said, 'but since no one thinks the narrator can be the killer, isn't it the same kind of fraud?'

'You haven't read my story,' I said. 'I haven't handed it in yet, so how can you say that?' He argued that if a renowned writer like S. S. Van Dine, a classic, had gone to the trouble of showing how a detective novel is done, why not follow it to the letter?

'S. S. Van Dine also says here that it's forbidden to discover the identity of the killer through a cigarette butt left at the scene of the crime,' I said. 'Take a look, it's in writing. And we can't use the-dog-that-doesn't-bark-because-he-knows-the-killer either. Also, forest rangers, cooks and the like shouldn't be the guilty party. We've done that over and over again,' I said.

'The dog that doesn't bark? Who did that?' he asked. 'Tell me and I'll give him the boot this very day.'

'Our entire collection is full of cigarette butts and murderous butlers,' I replied.

'A dog that doesn't bark, that we don't have,' he said, and continued: 'I can't read all the books they give me. If it's written that murderous butlers are forbidden, that's that. They're forbidden. We have to follow the Americans' rules. Stop the book and begin a different one.'

'I've already written forty pages,' I said. 'It's not fair. You approved the outline.'

'I'm not going to argue with you. I want another outline on my desk by this afternoon. In seven days I want the finished book.'

'Seven days? That's impossible. I need two weeks, that's our deal.'

'You've already used up seven days writing that thing,' he said. 'I might point out that Simenon would write a book in a week. Edgar Wallace once wrote an entire novella in two days. Zé Negrão, of the Wild Horses of the West series, is writing one a week. Paulinho, of the Hail of Bullets series, does a shoot-'em-up in ten days. They're both dying to work with me. I'm the only one who pays on time. Cash on delivery. Am I lying? OK, then. That's it. You have to write. Sit down and write. That's what you've got to do. You can go now.'

'You're always in such a hurry,' said Ingrid, the secretary, when I passed by her desk. 'I'd like to talk to you. Any time. Can I call you one of these days?'

9

I arrived home in the middle of a battle between my mother, at the window, and the wife of the tenants' association president, with her steam machine and her habit of sterilizing the sidewalk. 'The filth isn't in the lamppost,' my mother was saying, 'it's in the soul. It does no good to clean the post if the conscience is stained.'

'Shut up, you crazy old biddy. And tell that son of yours to pay the back condo fees he owes.'

I took the megaphone from my mother's hands and led her away from the window.

'The one who rules my life is Jesus Christ. Damn them to the hell of sinners. Give me back my megaphone.'

My mother was especially bad that week. She would preach at the window, and the neighbors were complaining. 'If she's religious,' said my uncle Alberto, a doctor, when I called him for advice, 'if she believes in God, more power to her. You don't have the slightest idea what it's like to lose a son, the way she did. You don't have children, you don't know that kind of love. If she has God, good for her. God and money should be made use of while we have them,' he said. 'I remember one of those Nobel Prize winners telling about how he lost his faith. I read it in some magazine. The guy was in Auschwitz or some such place, and he witnessed a massacre of children. Where was God, someone asked. And a voice inside answered that God was hanging from the gallows. I never needed to see little children die to know that God doesn't exist,' Uncle Alberto said. 'I envy your mother. It's terrible with me. Not to believe in God doesn't mean not regretting the lack of God. I'm of the following opinion: a mother who can lose a twenty-two-year-old son to leukemia can face up to anything. I saw your mother beside the coffin, that is, I saw the pieces of her; the impression we had was that your mother was disintegrating before our very eyes. I couldn't stand pain like that, I prefer to die. I can't take coming to see you two anymore. Mercedes is always telling me, "Let's go over there, let's visit your sister. Rosário needs you." I can't bear seeing Rosário. I look at her and I see stamped on her forehead "I'm suffering like a rabid dog". It's shit.'

I gave my mother the tranquilizer that Uncle Alberto prescribed, then stayed in the room until she went to sleep.

I spent the rest of the afternoon waiting for Melissa, but she didn't show up until evening. She sat on my lap and turned off the computer. 'Look at what we've got here,' Melissa said, showing me a piece of paper with various notations. 'It wasn't easy,' she said. 'It took me three days to get this.'

We had several possibilities. Of them all, São Francisco Xavier, a small city an hour from São José dos Campos, struck us as the best. Melissa also had a friend who knew the area; the roads were pretty bad, she had told her, and very dangerous as well.

'Now for the most interesting part,' said Melissa. 'There's a hospital just at the entrance to São José. Read this: São Januário Hospital. Supply: zero. They've been without serum for eight months; I could hardly believe it when I saw it.

So, the snake attacks Ronald, we go to São Francisco, there's no serum there, we make a dash for São José, we run around like a chicken with its head cut off, looking for serum. Do you like my plan?'

I took Melissa to my bed. 'I like it,' I said. 'Take off that blouse.'

'Really, you like it?'

'I like it. Take off those pants.'

'You think it'll work?'

'Yes,' I said. 'Take it off.'

'I'm taking it off,' she said. 'I love it when you look at me like that.'

We made love until nightfall.

Later, in the restaurant, as we waited for our pizza, Melissa leafed through the *Get to Know Rural Brazil* tourist guide that we had bought at the newsstand near my house. 'Take a look at this,' she said, handing me the guide. I read the description of a country inn located in a small town eleven miles by dirt road from São Francisco Xavier. 'Unbelievable luck,' she said. 'We've found it. That's the place.'

We calculated that it would take approximately two hours for Ronald to receive the serum. Or more.

'I'll talk to him tomorrow,' Melissa said. 'It won't be easy to convince him. We've been fighting, and suddenly I invite him to spend a weekend in a hotel in the country. He'll think it strange.'

'It's normal,' I said. 'Couples do that. They fight and they make up.'

'I'll try. The bandage comes off Friday. If all goes well, we'll do the thing on Saturday. We have a week to prepare everything.'

'On Friday?' I asked.

'On Saturday.'

'I was talking about the bandage. I thought your arm would be immobilized for a month.'

The waiter brought the pizza.

'Yes,' she said. 'That would be the ideal. Let me serve you. The doctor explained that it wasn't a fracture, it was just – pepperoni only? – it was just – this smells very good – it was just a sprain. I can even drive.'

The pizza was lousy, a crummy sauce and a thick crust. I put my silverware on my plate.

'You told me it was a fracture,' I said.

'No,' she replied, 'it was a sprain. I remember perfectly telling you it was a sprain. The mozzarella is better, want to try it?'

'No.'

'I told you it wasn't a fracture, of course I told you, don't you remember?'

Funny, I didn't remember.

10

From: José Guber To: Wilmer da Silva

The Deadly Toad, by Joseph Farnsworth

I, William Mambler, at the age of twenty, left my job as karate instructor and went to work for the largest insurance company in California. My first client was a young, rich, good-looking guy who wanted to take out a policy for a million dollars. Policies that large require a series of medical exams, and the guy did them all. We verified that he was in excellent health and the contract was signed. Some months later, the man, whose name was Walter Nadenger, died of a heart attack. I found it very strange; nobody at the age of thirty-four takes out a life-insurance policy for a million dollars and dies a natural death shortly afterwards. I suggested that the company perform an autopsy on the cadaver. They claimed an autopsy could only be done in the case of accidental or culpable death, which was definitely not the case, since we had a death certificate signed by one of the most eminent doctors in California, assuring us that the cause of death was myocardial infarction.

I decided to go to the wake. The widow, one of those women who are all the time taking pills to kill their appetite and tranquilizers to keep from slapping the maids, was by herself, only her and the corpse. I thought that was strange, but I know that rich people are like that; they fight with the entire family over stock control of the father's company. Fine. I was in the courtyard of the cemetery, not the chapel, because obviously the widow wouldn't allow me to remain beside the deceased. So I watched everything from a distance. Suddenly, there was some confusion: a drunken biker, who was sitting by the body of his girlfriend in the adjoining chapel, was saying, 'That broad next door is feeding the body through a funnel.' They said he was drunk, but not even a drunk could make up such a ridiculous story.

The insurance payment was in fact made. I didn't give up. In the widow's apartment I found two things that piqued my suspicions: a small, foul-smelling plant with round leaves, and a dead toad. I looked up the Amphibian Protection Society. There I met a scientist who helped me greatly with the investigation. I discovered that the toad contains a series of hallucinogenic and anesthetic substances that can provoke a temporary shutdown in our nervous system. People under the effect of these drugs show no sign of life even though they are alive and retain certain functions, like memory for example. Scientifically, this phenomenon is known as zombiism, or deep catalepsy. When the zombie is fed a mixture of toad venom and the chemical substances of the *Pyrethrum parthenium* plant, the zombilike state is prolonged for several hours. (Another important point. The foul-smelling flower I found in the widow's apartment was *Pyrethrum parthenium*.) I put this information in my report to the insurance company, making it clear that in my view the company was the victim of fraud. They read the report and did absolutely nothing, ignoring it. In other words, they didn't believe my suspicions. If I were less ingenuous, I would have stopped there. But I was quite certain of what I was saying, and I decided to dig deeper. With the help of some friends, I ingested the mixture of toad venom and substances extracted from the plant and fell into a state of profound catalepsy. I was fed the anesthetic substance several times. Afterwards, my friends called a doctor, who examined me and signed my death certificate. Myocardial infarction. When I woke up, I took the death certificate to the company president. Know what he did? He took the certificate and ripped it into tiny pieces. He bought off the doctor who signed the certificate. And he fired me. The president of the company was involved in the scheme and came out very well, getting his cut of the million dollars.

The book ends with the protagonist renting an office in Hollywood. He hangs out a shingle that reads: William Mambler, Private Detective.

From: Wilmer da Silva To: José Guber

I have the impression that since you've forgotten how to tell a story you're increasing the size of your outlines. So I'm going to increase the size of my reply. I'm against using animals in crime fiction, although I appreciate that you're trying to take advantage of this ecological fad. I agree that we need to modernize the detective novel, bring in day-to-day issues like the Internet, ecology, sexual harassment, cloning, all that stuff. But using toads? All that's missing is for you to write a story about the killing of a golden lion tamarin, if there's still one alive. We're in favor of the ecology, but Minnesota isn't an NGO, get that through your head. Outline rejected. You have five days to hand in the book.

Melissa called from the intercom in the garage of my building, asking me to come downstairs; she wanted to show me a surprise. I went down. She showed me her arm without a bandage. 'I'm feeling great,' she said, 'I'm cured.' She opened the trunk, took out a box; inside was a brown rattlesnake, dark with diamond-shaped markings on its back, a yard or less in length. '*Crotalus durissus,*' she said, showing me the serpent. 'With a milliliter of the venom from this *durissus* we could kill thirty thousand pigeons.'

'I thought we were going to use a *jararaca,*' I said.

'We were,' she replied. 'A crate happened to arrive at the Institute today, and I was the first to get my hands on it. No one knows exactly how many specimens we received. And they're not going to find out.'

Melissa asked to leave the rattler in my bedroom. I didn't like the idea. It was one thing to have a boa constrictor beside my bed; a rattlesnake was completely different. It bothered me to some extent. I couldn't sleep well.

From the very start I had a bad feeling. The rattlesnake wouldn't eat, wouldn't drink any water, and practically wouldn't move. When Melissa picked it up, it didn't try to escape or even become alert, like my boa. I began to think the rattler was sick. I'd read somewhere that extremely apathetic serpents could be suffering from a respiratory infection. I told this to Melissa. 'No,' she said, 'it's normal. When snakes change habitats they refuse food and change their behavior. In the Calcutta zoo a serpent went on a hunger strike just because they added something new to his diet. That's how snakes are.'

I had my doubts. 'What if when push comes to shove,' I said, 'this depressed snake doesn't do a decent job?'

Melissa, reacting to my advice, brought a chicken to my

apartment. 'Let's test the *durissus*,' she said, releasing the animal in the bedroom.

I expected to see one of those scenes from a National Geographic program, with the serpent preparing for its attack, its forked tongue vibrating menacingly, its rattles foretelling tragedy, and finally the pounce. That wasn't how it happened. The chicken didn't approach the snake or vice versa. Several times, Melissa placed the prey beside the rattlesnake. Nothing happened. I noticed that Melissa was holding the bird too tightly. I heard the sound of the chicken's neck snapping. Melissa threw it on the floor, stomped it, staining my bedroom floor. 'Have you gone nuts?' I asked. The rattler pounced and seized the lifeless chicken in its jaws. At that instant my mother came into the room, saw the serpent swallowing the chicken, its beak still outside.

'What kind of witchcraft is this?' my mother asked. I tried to explain, but she refused to listen. 'Get this young woman out of here,' she said. 'I saw the chicken, I saw the snake, I saw the blood. I'm not a fool, don't explain anything. I know very well what that is,' she said, 'it's the devil. That woman will bring misfortune to our family.'

In the midst of the confusion Ingrid, Wilmer's secretary, called me. I thought it was to nag me about outlines, but she wanted to invite me to dinner, or for coffee if dinner was too complicated. I couldn't imagine what that persistent blonde wanted from me, but in any case I tried to get out of it. 'I really need to talk to you,' she said. 'It's important.'

We agreed to meet at eight o'clock, in a bar near my place. I put away the snake, cleaned up the floor, accompanied Melissa to her car, and went to meet Ingrid.

I got there twenty minutes early. It was the type of place I hated, a small bar full of, as they say, enthusiastic drinkers. I asked for a table and sat there observing the zoo. The disgust those people aroused in me was amazing. The women were better; at least they didn't laugh loudly. Nothing but paunchy types around; having a paunch was the norm. And take the couples. You can tell how long a couple's been together just by watching the way they behave at a table. After three years they don't even look at each other.

Ingrid was wearing a tight T-shirt, her arms bare; only that day did I notice that her eyes were blue. She sat down and said she'd like a mineral water. She said she was very objective and fast. And that she hated sluggish people. 'I'll say what I have to say right off,' she said. 'I've heard rumors at the office. They're going to fire you. I shouldn't be telling you anything; we hardly know each other. But I've liked you since that very first day. I know you have a sick mother. My mother was sick too. She died, my mother. That's the only reason I'm telling you this. That's all I have to say.'

We walked to her place, exchanging pleasantries. When we got to the door of her building, she asked if I wanted to come in, said we could have a drink.

Ingrid was very attractive. I thought it best not to accept. A man either takes a woman to bed or leaves her alone.

11

From: José Guber To: Wilmer da Silva
Wilmer, pay attention, this is a long outline. Be patient. Don't skip any part of it or you won't understand my objective. OK, here we go.
The Animal, by Peter Walpole (I like the name, but I also thought of Sol Greene, if you want something less gothic)

Extraordinary crimes
Two women, mother and daughter, killed in brutal fashion. The daughter is strangled and stuck upside down in the chimney of her house. The body of the mother (who was thrown out the apartment window) shows multiple wounds. The head was practically severed from the body.

Duque, the investigator
Wilmer, to give an idea of the deductive capabilities of this formidable detective that I've created, I plan to write an introductory scene, something like this:

Duque and his sidekick Remarq are walking along the streets of London, or New York, whichever you prefer. They're walking in silence, absorbed in thought, just as Aristotelians do.

'Do you think the actor John Malcolm ought to be on

television?' asks Duque. His assistant Remarq is astonished to see that his friend is capable of guessing his thoughts. At that exact moment he had been thinking that John Malcolm wasn't a good enough actor for the theater.

'How did you know that I was thinking exactly about J. Malcolm?'

'Because of the fruit vendor who bumped into you when we turned the corner. You lost your balance and looked with irritation at the cobblestones. I saw that you said the word stereotomy to yourself, referring to that type of pavement. One who's thinking of stereotomy thinks of atoms and, as a logical consequence, in the theories of Epicurus. I recalled that in a conversation we had a few days ago about that subject we said that several of Epicurus's assumptions had been borne out by nebular cosmology. One who thinks of nebular cosmology looks at the sky and seeks out the great nebula in Orion, which is exactly what you did. You looked upward. It occurred to me that in their criticism of Malcolm's work, the newspapers made reference to the verse *Perdidit antiquum litera sonum,* which, as we've already said, refers to Orion. It wasn't difficult to deduce that you were establishing a connection between these two things: Orion and Malcolm. You smiled, whereupon I remembered the inexpressive figure of Malcolm and deduced what you were thinking: Malcolm is a mediocre actor who's not right for the theater. Simple, isn't it?'

Wilmer, this is an example of the deductive abilities of my character.

The investigation

Duque, upon investigating the double homicide, quickly discovers that:

- The assassin grunted. (A conclusion based on statements from witnesses who on the night of the crime heard someone speaking Russian, Czech, Slovenian, Tupi-Guarani and other weird languages, in the victims' apartment. In other words, the murderer spoke a language unknown to all of them.)
- To reach the window of the victims' apartment, the murderer used the wire connected to the lightning rod. (Like a monkey leaping from branch to branch.)
- The murderer did not steal the four thousand dollars that was in the apartment. (This is not a human behavior pattern.)
- Animal fur is found in the victims' hands. (An animal?)
- The excoriation marks were not made by human hands. (What animal?)
- The hairs found in the victims' hands are the same as those of tawny orang-utans found on the islands of the East Indies.

The strategy of capture
Duque publishes in the newspaper the following notice: 'Captured a Bornean orang-utan. For further information, come to street such-and-such, number such-and-such (Duque's address).'

Denouement
A sailor comes looking for Duque, claiming to be the owner of the orang-utan. Pressed by the detective, he confesses that:

He had been traveling in Borneo lately and had bought a baby orang-utan. He had brought it to London and left it locked in a cage. He was waiting for the animal to heal from a wound in the foot to sell it to the zoo. One night, however, the orang-utan escaped. The sailor chased it, saw it climb up the lightning-rod wire and into a building. Upon entering the apartment that the orang-utan had gone into, he saw, terrified, the mother and daughter being brutally killed by the beast. He fled in fear, leaving the beast loose in the city.

The sailor is freed immediately after the necessary statements to the police. Later, the orang-utan is captured by the sailor himself, who sells it to the zoo. And thus we come to the end of the story.

From: Wilmer   To: José Guber
Your stories are getting longer and longer in length and shorter and shorter in talent. A good story is one whose theme can be told in a few words, like Goethe's *Faust*: a guy sells his soul to the devil and fucks up. See the conciseness? Send another one. You've got two days.

When you decide to kill a guy, it's good to know, the worst phase is the preparation. It's as if every nerve in your body were being stretched to its breaking point. The details are rough. You have to think of everything, especially the lies you'll be telling afterwards and the way you'll be telling them. What looks easy is hard, and what looks hard is even harder. We thought it would only be a problem to get Ronald to go to a hotel in the country; it was a real battle. He wanted to go to the seashore. 'I don't like the mountains,' he said, 'I like the beach. I hate mud, I hate cows, what's there to do in a place like that?' Melissa was even thinking of changing the scenario, but snakes and beaches make for a very implausible combination, and she insisted so much, repeating the same thing over and over, that Ronald finally agreed from sheer exhaustion.

My part in the crime was planned in minute detail. My function would be to appear on the scene as savior and complicate everything, making the trip to São José total hell, delaying to the maximum the application of the serum.

Thanks to Melissa, the theoretical part of the plan was going well. Hotel, maps, everything OK, reservations, supplies of serum, everything was minutely checked.

What caused the most problems was the rattlesnake. When it came to attacking and eating, it didn't show the slightest enthusiasm. For several days we threw mice into the pen, and nothing. Everything was set for Friday; we didn't have much more time. 'Let's try chicks,' Melissa said. We tried yellow chicks. Nothing. Toads. Nothing. Wednesday, Thursday, time was running out. 'Take it easy,' Melissa said, 'it's just scared.' More chickens, nothing, white rabbit, nothing, half-dead rabbit, more mice. Actually we had to take the mice out of the pen; otherwise they'd take over.

On Friday Melissa agreed with me. 'This snake won't work,' she said, 'we have to get a different one.'

'Steal another one,' I said.

'It'd be impossible to steal another serpent from the Institute,' Melissa explained. 'The new crates had already been catalogued. If we do that, we'll be taking chances.'

A scientific crime is always very laborious. It's not for nothing that killers prefer to settle the matter with automatics.

12

Melissa had heard of a clandestine serpentarium in Atibaia, a little over forty miles from São Paulo. She made a few calls and found out its location. The car was almost out of gasoline; we had to fill up as we left São Paulo. 'Leave the windshield,' she told the attendant, 'we're in a hurry.'

In less than an hour we were at Esperança Farm. We were met by a red-nosed guy who either had a cold or an allergy and was called Lelé. The serpents were in a small building, enclosed by several screens, next to the farm's office. Lelé held the snakes by the neck and wanted us to see the fangs that injected the venom. He showed us a two-year-old *jararaca.* 'This animal,' he said, 'is the devil himself.'

That was the one we bought. 'Do you have toads here?'

We returned to São Paulo. Melissa left me at my place; she was very calm. There was a fax from Wilmer on my table. Without reading it, I wadded it up and threw it in the trash. I made a light meal for my mother, explained that I'd be away for two days and that Aunt Mercedes was coming to keep her company.

I took a shower, dressed, packed a suitcase. At two o'clock I was at the car-rental agency near my apartment. I chose the car with the cheapest daily rate. I put the suitcase and the box with the *jararaca* and toad in the trunk and got onto the highway. I arrived in São Francisco before 5 p.m. A small town lost in the middle of the mountains, completely without charm. Just looking at it got me down. I turned onto the dirt road; it was far worse than we had imagined. I really detested it, the little houses, mud, chickens, pigs, straw hats, ignorance and goodness, it all made me feel enormously sad.

The hotel was a former coffee plantation with an enormous old house, where the more comfortable and more expensive rooms were, and some concrete boxes of the hell-with-you type that they called chalets, scattered through the woods. The manager, Dona Iolanda, was a plump, fortyish woman with dark skin and bleached blonde hair. Women of that type shouldn't bleach their hair; the contrast of blonde and dark skin gives them a pitiable look. I've never understood why women change the color of their hair. I asked if I could select my room.

She thought that because I was from the city I would want silence and offered me an apartment off by itself. I explained that my problem was exactly the opposite. I was tired of solitude and wanted to see human beings. That turned her on, I could see. She asked if I liked to dance and what kind of music I liked. Through that kind of idle talk I discovered that the hotel only had seven guests and that Melissa and Ronald would be staying in Apartment 8. I installed myself in Apartment 9.

I called home and retrieved the messages from the answering machine. Wilmer had phoned twice. I filled the tub and took a leisurely bath, just to kill time.

Night in São Francisco was just that, black night and nothing else. From the porch of my bedroom I couldn't even see the trees a few yards away. The smell of the forest even came in through my eyes, an impressive thing. I heard when Melissa arrived with Ronald; I heard everything, in fact, that they said while they arranged their things, and they weren't fighting. He was speaking to Melissa delicately: 'Did you bring my racket, dear?'

Actually, she was the one who was brusque with him. 'I brought it, I brought your racket,' she said in an irritated tone.

'Do you have to answer like that?' he said.

'It's the third time you've asked about the racket,' she said. 'You don't listen when I talk.'

I could even hear the toilet flushing.

I was the first to arrive at the restaurant. Dona Iolanda was on the telephone, but she made an effort to hang up quickly in order to better smother me with her enthusiasm and kindness. Two couples came in, the women in the lead, tight clothes, happy, long hair, the men in polo shirts.

Melissa and Ronald were the last to come in. I was the only one there who wasn't wearing a polo shirt. If I'd known, I'd have brought one.

The entire time, Ronald acted in a pleasant manner. He was attentive, he ate, said things, laughed. The other two couples, the same.

I went back to my room and turned on the television. The reception was awful. I turned it off. Melissa phoned me.

'Ronald went to the office to send a fax,' she said.

'He doesn't seem to be rough with you.'

'In front of others he's always like that.'

'Did you check to see if they have the serum?'

'I checked just to be on the safe side,' she said. 'I knew they didn't have it. For some time now the Institute has only been supplying public-health clinics. He's coming back, I'd better get off the phone.'

I spent the rest of the night tossing in bed.

13

On Saturday, I put on my trunks and went to the pool. The two couples were already there, four lizards stretched out in the sun, anointing themselves with suntan lotion. One of them was wearing the cover-the-whole-face type of sunglasses and seemed to want to make people say, hey, man, I see you have one righteous pair of sunglasses.

Melissa was late in arriving. A black one-piece bathing suit and a hat, I liked what I saw. Ronald put on a real show, diving into the pool and swimming for over half an hour, crawl, backstroke, butterfly. Moisés, my brother, swam much better than him. Funny how I never could remember Moisés talking, swimming, or doing things he enjoyed; I only remembered him in the hospital dying, hairless from the chemotherapy, writhing in pain. Once, after getting morphine, he told me that he always dreamed he was swimming. 'When you swim in the ocean,' he said, 'you're alone in the world, it's a feeling of fullness, you and the liquid immensity. You don't feel fatigue, you feel only that you're a part of all that, of the universe, you feel that everything is harmonious, everything is right.'

I became depressed thinking about my brother. I got into the pool and floated, looking at the sky.

I spent the rest of the day in my room. I started getting

nervous around five o'clock, after storing the *jararaca* and the toad in the trunk of my car, where Melissa would get them while Ronald was taking a bath.

At dinner, Melissa was quite tense. The two inseparable couples were still inseparable, and in polo shirts. The only time they took off the polo shirts was to go in the pool. The two women might be sisters; they looked a lot alike and could be described in five words: white clothes, bangs, red fingernails. No, six words: chubby. They liked to eat, the slugs. When it was time for dessert, without any remorse they asked for chocolate and ice-cream, and the fatter of the two even attacked her husband's dessert. It's impressive how those women eat and put on weight; just take a look around us, everybody overweight. They invited me to sit with them.

Melissa didn't like it. She shot me a furious look when she crossed the salon with Ronald.

The two couples were saying, 'We like bridge a lot, we're spending Carnival in Bahia, we love to jet ski.' The only one saying 'I' was me. Before I went to my room, just after Melissa left, one of the women said to me, 'We'd like to know something that's been intriguing us since yesterday. Why did you come to the hotel all by yourself?' I answered that I enjoyed solitude and one of them said that they had been intrusive.

I laughed. 'Not intrusive, not at all,' I said. 'You were very kind to invite a man by himself to have dinner with you, very kind. I like solitude,' I said, 'but once in a while it's good to make a change. Human beings,' I said. I think I'd had too much to drink.

'We're from Valinhos,' they explained. With those bangs, I thought, there was no need to explain. Valinhos. I went to my room, my head full of wine, I shouldn't have drunk so much. I lay down and, somehow or other, went to sleep.

I woke up with Melissa nudging me. 'What happened?' I asked.

'Keep your voice down,' she said. 'I think I overdid the tranquilizer. The snake already bit him. But he didn't wake up.'

'How can that be?' I asked.

'I don't understand it either,' she said. 'He should be feeling sick. I'm going to wait a while longer, we'll gain some time. I'll go into the bathroom and yell when I come out. He'll wake up, and you'll do what we planned.'

That's what I did. I waited in bed for ten minutes; I was feeling dizzy. I heard Melissa scream and went to the room next door, knocked on the door. No one answered. Did Melissa really scream, I wondered, or did I doze off and dream she was screaming? No, I thought, she had screamed. I heard the cries. I knocked again, nothing. I turned the knob, went in, and as I did, woke up Ronald.

'Who are you?' he asked, jumping out of bed and putting on his sandals. He was wearing striped pajamas.

'I heard someone call for help,' I said.

'Who called for help?' he asked.

Melissa came out of the bathroom, wearing a jersey, her hair wet.

'What's going on?' she asked.

'This man,' Ronald replied, 'this man came in here saying he'd heard someone yell for help.'

'I did hear someone yell for help,' I said. 'I don't know if it was here.'

'It might have been the TV,' Melissa said.

'It could have come from outside,' Ronald said.

Ronald didn't show any signs of pain, nothing; he was acting perfectly normally.

'You'll excuse me, but I clearly heard someone asking for help,' I said.

'We can phone the office,' Ronald suggested.

'No,' Melissa said.

'Why not?' Ronald asked. 'We don't see anything here,' he said, 'and it may be that someone is having a problem.'

'You're right,' I said.

'Ronald,' he said, holding out his hand. 'Glad to meet you. Excuse the pajamas. Are you staying in Number 9?'

'Exactly,' I answered. 'My name is José Guber.'

'My wife, Melissa,' he said.

'A pleasure,' Melissa and I said.

'Shouldn't we phone the office?' I asked.

Melissa picked up the telephone, and then, unexpectedly, Ronald grabbed a chair and lifted it. I thought he was going to hit me, but with a quick gesture he brought it down on the head of the *jararaca*, which was beside the wardrobe, about to spring toward me.

'Look, Ronald. That *jararaca* came in here chasing that toad we found in the bathroom,' Melissa said, replacing the phone on the hook.

'We found a toad in the bathroom today,' Ronald told me, 'a huge toad. He was running away, poor thing.'

'It was about to attack me.' I said. 'You saved my life.'

Ronald went to the porch and Melissa and I followed. The darkness was total. Ronald began an inane discussion about mysticism and mediums. He believed that his deceased mother had possessed the power to foresee things. Once, for example, she had said she had dreamed about roses, and the next day Aunt Rosa had arrived. On another occasion she had dreamed about potatoes and immediately afterwards had inherited a potato farm from her great-aunt.

Then Ronald grimaced. 'I feel a pain in my foot,' he said.

'My God, Ronald,' Melissa said, 'you've been bitten. There are two puncture marks here. We need antitoxic serum, immediately.' She looked at me. 'Could you go to the hotel office? They may have serum.'

Dona Iolanda became nervous when she heard of the accident. 'I don't have any serum,' she said, her fat hands clutching her cheeks. 'There's never been an accident here. Never.' I went back to their room and communicated the fact that there wasn't any serum in the hotel and that I could take them to the nearest first-aid station.

'Put the *jararaca* in the car,' Melissa said.

My car didn't want to start. Melissa was extremely nervous; she really was, she wasn't faking. I was impressed by Ronald's self-control. 'You two are really nervous; it's just a snakebite. I'll get the serum and I'll be fine,' he said. But when we got to São Francisco and were informed that there wasn't any serum, he began to sweat, and moan, and later, when I stopped the car at the side of the road, saying we had a flat tire, the man cried, actually cried, said he didn't want to die, and things got worse. 'I don't want to be separated from you, Tica,' he said. Tica was the affectionate nickname Ronald had given to Melissa, and she called him Tico.

'Take it easy, Tico, you're going to be all right.'

Ronald vomited in the car as I was changing the tire. Melissa stuck her head out the window.

'Tica,' I said.

'I've never seen such strong venom,' she replied, whispering.

At 12:15 a.m., we were at the hospital in São José. Ronald was taken away by nurses. Shortly afterwards, a doctor came to inform us that Ronald had gone into a coma.

14

To: Wilmer From: José Guber
The Depraved Epileptic, by Keith Findley
(Wilmer, the character will be inspired by Lombroso's criminal. We'll set the story in the nineteenth century, since the theme has to do with the scientific thought of the time.)

Diogo, a locomotive engineer, is a failed born criminal, since he's never killed anybody, except for a cat, which he kicked to death. He has a Lombrosian skull and suffers from a form of epilepsy that negatively influences his behavior. His problem: his ancestral hatred of women, a hatred that comes from the successive betrayals suffered by men, from the time they lived in caves and prehistoric women took advantage of the moments when the men were off hunting deer, or fighting, to betray them. (Wilmer: another title just occurred to me: *The Cursed Heritage*.)

Eva, a young newlywed, pretty and sensual, kills, with the help of her husband, her godfather the millionaire Ernest (whose heir she is) on a train trip. Diogo, the engineer, witnesses the crime. A bloody bond is created between them. Diogo falls in love with the murderess, not for her beauty or her qualities but precisely because she is a murderess. (Wilmer, I thought about creating the following parallel: Eva's crime is the work of art; she, the killer, is the artist, and he is the potential artist, experiencing the torment of creation.) One day, Eva confesses her crime (the secrets of her art) to Diogo, who upon hearing the details of the murder (the work of art) gets up the courage to kill Eva, thus realizing a work of his own. Final scene: Diogo, the engineer, being killed by one of Eva's admirers in the gears of the train.

Cordially, Guber

From: Wilmer To: José Guber
What is it with you? Have you been hitting some shrink's couch?

The outline of *The Depraved Epileptic* went into the trash. Your time is up.

I want to talk to you.

Give Yourself a Hand

I DECLARE that, in order to live, you must arm yourselves with eyes from head to foot: not merely with eyeholes in your armature but with enormous eyes, open and awake. Eyes in your ears, to discover so much falsity, so many lies; eyes in your hands, to see what others give and, more important, what they take; eyes in your arms, to measure your capabilities; eyes on your tongue, to think what to say; eyes in your chest, to help to develop patience; eyes in your heart, to protect you from first impressions; eyes in your very eyes, to see how they are seeing.

Baltasar Gracián
El Criticón

15

It's one thing for you to stick a knife in somebody's back and something else, completely different, to facilitate the job of a serpent. It was a crime all the same, but the fact is that I didn't feel like a murderer. I was perfectly OK, no remorse, I was calm, driving peacefully along the Dutra highway, feeling nothing but a bit of sleepiness. I stopped at a gas station and had some coffee. When I returned to the car, I noticed that I had forgotten the dead *jararaca* in the back seat. I threw it on the side of the road.

Melissa had said that Ronald would die in less than eight hours. She had notified his family, his cousins, and they would be arriving at any minute. We thought it better for me to return to São Paulo. We agreed that I wouldn't go to the wake or the funeral; Melissa would keep me informed of everything by phone.

In São Paulo, the first thing I did was return the car to the rental agency. I stopped by a bakery and bought a box of assorted chocolates for my mother. I also bought, at a pet store, two baby mice for my boa.

There were a lot of messages on the answering machine. Most of them were from Wilmer nagging me about work.

I took a shower, lay down on the bed, and waited. According to my calculations, Ronald should already be dead. But he wasn't. In the intensive care ward, full of tubes and needles stuck all over his body, Ronald was surviving. His lungs were being operated by a respirator and his heart, which had already stopped once, was still functioning thanks to cardioversion. That's what Melissa told me on the phone. 'I'm dying to see all this over with,' she said. 'I want to marry you.'

On Monday I went to the publishing house, very early. My deadline had passed, but I could ask for an extension, I could ask for another week, I could ask for an advance; that was what I had in mind. 'You're not answering your phone these days?' Wilmer asked as soon as he saw me.

My appearance must not have been all that good. Wilmer smiled. That was when I understood. I'd been in that bind for two years, and the day had finally arrived. I didn't return the smile. 'Care for some coffee?' he asked. 'Ingrid, two coffees, please. Well then? You didn't come through?'

'No, I didn't come through.'

Ingrid approached with two disposable cups.

'I understand what's happening to you,' Wilmer continued. 'It's known as a creative crisis. I thought that you were one of the very few able to bear up under the agonies of creation. Writing is hell. Any profession is better. Garbage collector, for instance. Sometimes I see the guy in the rain, climbing up on that truck loaded with crap, and think: That poor devil has Saturdays and Sundays. Nobody knows writers the way I do. The only book you guys write without any problem is the first one. On the second one, you face the crisis of seeing if you're really writers or if everything was just spilling your guts. On the third novel comes the crisis of style. On the fourth, the crisis of searching for the style of the first book. It's like marriage – one crisis after another. The advantage to marriage is that it ends. I've been working with writers for ten years and I can testify that you suffer like hell. Paulinho last year called me late at night saying that he didn't know how to write. Now there he is, producing the best shoot-'em-ups we publish. You're in a crisis. That's not a problem. I always liked your books a lot, you've got a good text, you've got lots of style, I'm always saying that. But you don't have the necessary adrenaline.'

I saw right away that the fucker was going to fire me. 'The necessary adrenaline, you understand me? Some have it, some don't, that's all there is to it,' he said. I understood his game from the moment he offered me coffee. He never offered me coffee. Wilmer was delighting in the anticipated pleasure of firing me. There's a type of cretin whose greatest enjoyment comes from saying, 'You're fired,' to a subordinate. 'But you have many good qualities,' he said. 'You don't have adrenaline, but you make up for it by –'

'Listen, Wilmer,' I interrupted. I wasn't going to let him have his little pleasures. 'I don't want to work here anymore; have them figure out what you owe me.'

'What?' he asked, surprised. His perplexed voice trying to seem amiable, he said, 'I was going to invite you to be editor of the new magazine we're launching in two months, *Make Your Own Hope Chest.* You know that we're having good sales with *Make Your Own Clothes* and *Make Your Own Cosmetics.* This do-it-yourself thing is at a fever pitch. We're going to launch *Make Your Own Ice-Cream* and *Make Your Own Nest Egg.* Are you sure you want to leave?'

I felt like hitting myself in the face.

'Don't you want to give it some thought? Think about the salary. It's a good salary. And you won't have to write.'

'No,' I said. 'I want what's owed me.'

I thought he was going to insist. How was I to know? Wilmer concluded that I wouldn't back down. But the fucker concluded wrong, and in the end I was the one who fucked himself.

'Talk to Fuinha in Accounting,' he said, picking up the phone. 'I'll tell him you're coming by.'

That's life. Unemployed, crazy about a woman who raised snakes, waiting for a guy to die, no money, no prospects, and with a mother at home who was getting crazier by the minute. And acting proud. That's it.

16

Melissa didn't call Monday afternoon. That night, I went to the newsstands and bought some newspapers. Nothing. It wasn't possible for a news item like that not to be in the papers. I knew newspapers from my days as a proofreader; news like that beat automobile accidents, for example, by an order of magnitude. I remember the boy who was almost eaten by a crocodile; they loved that kind of stuff. They spent a week talking about crocodiles, interviews with the doctors who treated the kid, his parents, the kid himself, and, even better for circulation, the accident took place in Miami to boot; Brazil loves Miami. It was a real carnival.

Ronald was still alive; that was what the newspapers' silence told me. Some people linger before dying.

When I got home, there was no message from Melissa. Only Ingrid had phoned offering to introduce me to a self-help publisher. I thought about calling to thank her, but I didn't want to tie up the line in case Melissa called. I hadn't given that girl, Ingrid, much thought, and yet she was worried about me, telephoned me, wanted to know about me and find me a job.

The next few days were the same crap. Deaths. The children, grandchildren, and daughters-in-law of Ruth dos Santos announce her passing on the 1st. Alice Alves, ninety, widow. She leaves behind children. José Eustáquio Martins de Souza, widower. Rafael Scon. Nineteen cadavers. Everyone was dying but Ronald. I read the obituaries every morning, before reading the classified ads. I would begin the day irritated. Melissa didn't call. At the hospital, the woman who answered the phone didn't vary from the script: the patient's medical condition remains unchanged, sir.

I didn't leave the apartment. I read, sitting beside the phone, waiting, watching TV, eating junk, my money running out.

On Thursday I couldn't stand waiting any longer. 'Wanted: writer of erotic tales. Good pay.' I picked up the newspaper and went to do something about my life.

17

The magazine *Without Shame* belonged to an Argentine named Santamaria. They gave me a copy to read while I waited in the outer office. I leafed through it. The usual meat-and-potatoes, vaginas, penises, coitus and cunnilingus.

Santamaria received me in his office, looking me over suspiciously. My appearance maybe wasn't all that good. I noticed that he avoided shaking my hand. 'All our writers do their work right here,' Santamaria said. 'The hours are from noon to eight o'clock. I don't allow them to take work home. Or photos. We work in suits and ties. It's forbidden to use vulgar language in the editorial area.'

He handed me a file with photos of a black dwarf having sex with a blonde.

'I realize you're experienced, but we'll still have to analyze your text. It's a simple test. All you have to do is write a story about these photos. Sixty lines at most.'

We went to the editorial area. Three young men in suits and ties were sitting at typewriters. 'You can use this one here,' Santamaria told me, pointing to an Olivetti electric. As soon as he left, one of the writers asked to see my photos.

'You can take this and run with it,' he said. 'Know how your story ought to go? You got to have one fuck scene after another. That's the rule. Have you chosen your pseudonym?'

I didn't do too badly. I wrote a love story about a circus dwarf and a virgin ticket-seller who, at night after everyone had gone to sleep, go into the lions' cage to make love.

'Bocage Manuel – that's your pseudonym?' asked the editor when he got my text at the end of the day.

'Yes,' I said, 'but it can be changed.'

Santamaria read the story, silent, clearing his throat from time to time, and said he'd phone me as soon as he'd made a decision. He didn't call; neither did Melissa.

The next day, I awoke to the sound of the doorbell. I looked at the clock, 8 a.m. The torture was over, Ronald was dead. It's Melissa, I thought, who else would ring my doorbell at eight in the morning? Now, I thought, leaping out of bed, now comes the easy part, the wake, burial, it's over. I opened the door. 'Good morning,' said the head of the tenants' association. 'Sorry to bother you, but I need a minute of your time.' I felt a sense of discouragement; I knew exactly what had brought that short, ordinary-looking man to my place. I invited him in.

'We're very grateful for what your mother did with the street vendors,' he said. 'She put a stop to illegal trade on our street. But as to the sermons, please understand, I'm in favor of order. Though I'm Catholic, not a practicing one, I believe we shouldn't impose our religion on others. Besides which, your mother is not, shall we say, an ecclesiastic authority, so to speak. In the eyes of God, I mean, of the Church, no offense intended, your mother is a nobody. I'm sure you agree. Who is your mother to be preaching the word of God?'

He even took advantage of the occasion to dun me about my back condominium fees.

'That man has his nerve,' my mother said when I told her about the visit. 'He means that selling fruit is fine, steam-cleaning machines are fine, knife-sharpeners are fine, car horns are fine, everything is fine. But the word of God no one wants to hear. Go there and tell that maid-fornicator that I won't stop. I take my orders from God.'

I spent the day thinking about going out to look for work, with the newspaper open to the classifieds. Nothing but crap. As far as sitting beside the telephone and staring at the floor is concerned, I was a success. Time didn't pass. I decided to put an end to it. Two-thirty. I scooped up all the books that were on the floor and started putting them in the bookcase in alphabetical order. Then I cleaned up my worktable, scrubbed my computer keyboard with cotton swabs, used isopropyl alcohol on the monitor screen, and organized my papers. Three-thirty. I got the dirty clothes from the hamper, put detergent in the washing machine, washed and dried everything. That took another half-hour. The rest of the day I lay down, with the telephone at my side.

That night, after fixing my mother's dinner and washing dishes, I didn't know what more to do with myself. I couldn't stand that thing boiling inside me. We kill a guy and she doesn't even call me to say he died. Could she be at the wake? A wake takes a lot of work, I thought, the preparation, washing the body, dressing it, the flowers, the burial. I never bought that shopworn excuse that there wasn't a chance to phone. A woman in love leaves her husband in the coffin, by himself, and goes off to phone her lover. I'm going to call, I thought. I picked up the telephone. I don't care, I'm going to phone the hospital, I'm going to call Melissa in the hospital and ask for an explanation. When I took the phone off the hook I realized it was dead.

I went to the public telephone at the corner and called the phone company. 'It was disconnected because of lack of payment,' they said.

I called the hospital and asked for Melissa. She took a long time to come to the phone. Her voice was distant; she said she couldn't talk. I began to yell. 'You're going to talk, lady,' I yelled, 'you're going to tell me everything. I'm going crazy here with no information.'

'Calm down,' she said.

'Calm down, my ass,' I shouted. 'Spill it right now unless you want me showing up at that crappy hospital.'

She said that Ronald had come out of the coma and was out of danger. 'What the shit kind of *jararaca* was that?' I asked, and the stupid-looking woman waiting behind me to use the phone stared at me, wide-eyed. 'I'm going to be on for some time, find another phone,' I told her.

'Melissa?' I said. 'Hello?'

'I can't talk now,' Melissa replied. 'Ronald is going into surgery, they're going to amputate his leg. Don't tie up the phone. Don't go out of the apartment. I'll call you.'

I went home. This was getting worse and worse. I felt enormously unhappy. Crippling someone, goddamn, that was playing dirty.

18

I explained to the guy that a snake like that was priceless, first because no one was dumb enough to go around offering a boa constrictor for sale; you'd be better off caught with ten kilos of cocaine, I said, than caught selling an animal from our protected fauna. They knew very well that it was an unbailable crime. I explained what I had already spent on nurslings, mice, veterinarians, equipment. 'In reality,' I said, 'this snake is priceless, but I'll sell it for three hundred dollars.'

We were in the rear of the pet shop. I was trying to convince the owner to buy my boa. He offered two hundred. I put the boa back in its box. 'Two-fifty is as high as I can go,' he said. I accepted.

I could do without anything, food, a bed, snakes, work, water, anything, but my telephone had to be working. Melissa was going to call at any moment, she'd said she would call. I went by the telephone company and paid my bill. I then called the publisher and asked Ingrid if her offer to find me a job was still open.

It wasn't the first time I'd heard of Universalis, the publisher of self-help books, where Ingrid's friend Mirna worked as a secretary.

Mirna, wearing a tight, baby-pink tailored suit that displayed her plump figure, and sweetish perfume, showed me around the publishing house, and as far as copying the style of the Americans went, I'd never seen anything like it. Except for Mirna's small office, which was mahogany and leather, the rest was six-foot-square cubicles where the salespeople worked. On the walls were dozens of posters with sayings relating to professional success. Of every ten words from Mirna, eight were Jequitibá, the major writer for the house.

Various of Pedro Jequitibá's books were displayed on shelves in the reception area. *Achieving Success and Power* (a stimulating work that will transform you into a successful professional). *Interacting with My Self* (a kit with video and two books about his spiritual essence and the power of his self, mental hygiene, money, success, power, and work). *What to Do to Make It to the Top.* On all the covers there was a photo of a smiling Pedro Jequitibá, a man of mixed blood, the type of person that you can't tell whether he was born in Korea or Roraima. The introductory text was always the same, tips on personal and professional success. The idea of progressing and doing well in life was at the heart of Pedro Jequitibá's business, something he made very clear. In fact, that was also the philosophy of the publishing house. To them, a book was more or less like a blender or any other household appliance, useful, something that should bring immediate benefit.

'This country is a warehouse of cretins,' said Ingrid, who was waiting with me in the reception area. 'The people read nothing but shit; no one wants to read poetry, they want *Achieving Success and Power.* Seven hundred thousand copies, forty-six printings. I have no doubt of it,' she said. 'Just look around you, everyone who passes by, in the street, here, anywhere, secretaries, executives, students, politicians, teachers, maids, fathers, mothers, everybody around us, the entire city, all of them cretins, a huge agglomeration of cretins, and those cretins, when they go into a bookstore, it's to buy the type of crap I'm holding in my hand. Seven hundred thousand copies. Almost a million. Doesn't it make you sick?'

To me, it was all OK as long as I got paid.

The first thing you saw when you entered the office of Laércio Arruda, the owner of Universalis, was a gigantic poster of Pedro Jequitibá. The man was a talking machine. He was very excited over an article he'd just read in the newspaper about the publication of manuals teaching how to steal, beg, and sell one's body to laboratories for scientific research. I ran my eyes over the material and read things like *Rent Your Body to Science* – all the tips for anyone who wants to make money as a test subject. *The Pocket Book for Those Who've Lost Their Jobs and Have to Beg* – tips on the best approaches to achieve the objectives: money (the principal one), shelter, food, tips on the best spots to work, and, finally, an analysis of the psychology of the giver ('fear and guilt are the beggar's best friends'). It didn't say exactly that; I'm adapting. There was a manual teaching the reader how to steal food from supermarkets by getting around the alarms and video cameras.

'We live in a country of con artists,' said Laércio. 'We've got a lot to say. How to cheat on your income tax. How to steal from your partner. How to steal electricity from the utility company or from the condo. Would you do such a thing? No, it's delirium, stupidity, an idea that crossed my mind. I talk while I think. Forget it. That kind of thing wouldn't catch on in Brazil. Our business is Pedro Jequitibá. Have you read his books? They're classics of self-help literature. We're about to launch a package of three fabulous titles. Jequitibá has always been concerned for all those people who have problems with self-affirmation. *Learn to Be Happy* is for those who won't embrace happiness. There are individuals who have a commitment to unhappiness; you must know some. For them, everything has to be unpleasant. If their children don't come for Sunday lunch they complain about loneliness, and if they do come they complain about having to fix lunch. The book will teach them to say, yes, I can, yes, I want to be happy, yes, I accept well-being, yes, I accept with pleasure making the spaghetti and washing the dishes, because I deserve a lunch with my children.'

The planned cover of *Learn to Be Happy* had, in Laércio's words, the Be Happy concept – which is to say they had shamelessly copied that idiotic smiley face.

'*Learn to Say No* is for a different reader,' Laércio said, 'the pathologically generous type, the guy who feels obliged to do anything they ask of him; you must have an aunt like that. And then there's *Learn to Say Maybe*, based on the Platonic concept by which the most important of virtues is the sense of measure, and the sense of measure is the mean. The philosophy of maybe is to think before acting. To doubt. To question. To be just. The reader learns to straddle the fence without ending up with egg on his face.'

Laércio didn't want to know anything about my résumé or my professional experience. He only asked if I had good grammar.

'Yes,' I said.

'What about syntax?'

'I can assure you,' I said, 'that my syntax is as good as my orthoepy.'

He seemed to like the reply. I was hired as a piecework proofreader, as Laércio made a point of emphasizing. 'You'll be Pedro Jequitibá's special reader. A freelancer with no benefits, understand? You'll like him a lot. An exceptional guy. I'll take you to his office.'

Pedro Jequitibá really wanted to write about angels. 'But there's a guy here in Brazil who already registered with the National Institute of Trademarks and Patents the exclusive use of the trademark "guardian angel". Real clever, that guy. I respect someone who gets there first,' he said. 'I'm thinking of patenting "self-love", "self-image", "self-affirmation" and other key words of self-help literature. In fact, just a minute, I want to jot this down, it's important, get a patent,' he told himself, writing some words in his notebook. 'There,' he said, 'to note down is to memorize. I note down everything.'

Pedro Jequitibá liked to talk about himself. He spoke to me of his friendship with the great Tibetan spiritual leader Yogi Maye Masheyeno, who first awakened his interest in 'useful metaphysical questions'; the words are those of Pedro himself. 'You know,' he said, 'there are existential questions that lead nowhere. I only deal with what's important, with what can lead to concrete objectives, professional accomplishments, profit, that's the issue.'

'Of course,' I said. In fact, 'of course' is all I said, along with 'yes', 'clearly', and 'doubtlessly', which seemed to stimulate Pedro Jequitibá. He went on and on relating details about his life and his good qualities.

Jequitibá handed me two diskettes with the *Learn to* trilogy that would soon be launched, for me to proof at home. 'I have a great facility for writing,' he told me. 'I sit down and write. It's as if something inside me were doing all the work. I'm just the vehicle. The things come, and all I have to do is put them down on paper, and that I do with the greatest of ease. Of course,' he added, 'there may be some spelling errors in the manuscript. I confess that spelling isn't my strong point.'

I left depressed. 'At least the salary's not as bad as what Wilmer paid you,' said Ingrid, trying to comfort me. It was no comfort.

19

When I left the publisher's, Ingrid invited me to have dinner at her place. I had promised Melissa I'd stay close to the phone; I thought of telling Ingrid no, but she'd been so kind, and I was truly grateful, so I accepted. We stopped at a supermarket and bought wine, lemons, and garlic.

She lived in a small apartment, with a flower-patterned sofa, ruffled curtains, and knick-knacks everywhere.

She put on an apron, opened the wine, and while I sat on a Formica-top stool beside the sink and drank, she kept moving back and forth in front of me, lighting the fire, talking, cutting things, laughing. It was becoming more interesting once the wine started to kick in.

During dinner, she told me she'd been married. She'd met the guy on a transatlantic cruise, Rio to Patagonia. They dated for four months, then got married. The man was simply sensational, Ingrid said. 'I was always saying,' she told me, "you just can't be this sensational," but the guy really was totally sensational. He liked to dance, liked restaurants, liked animals, liked the movies, theater, jazz, rock 'n' roll, bossa nova, and he cooked better than anybody you've ever met in your life. This pasta you're eating is his recipe. I would come home, tired, and he would take a salmon out of the freezer, open some wine, and stay in the kitchen singing.

When I sat down at the table, he would serve me a wonderful banquet. I forgot to mention that he was an engineer and made good money. Two months after the wedding, I come home and find my husband, that extraordinary man, six feet of pure muscle, in the bedroom. Picture the scene: a knife in his hand, his wrist slashed, bleeding. I simply didn't understand. He looked at me and wouldn't say a word. I took him to the hospital and called his family, and that's when they told me. My husband was a psychotic depressive. "Goddamn it," I screamed right there in the hospital, in front of his mother, his brothers and sisters, "how come nobody told me this before?"

' "We thought he had told you," they said. He was hospitalized, he got better, and then, every six months he would have an attack. He would be hospitalized, get better, get worse, better, worse, better, worse. The marriage lasted two years. One day, I came home, very unhappy, I opened the door, he was in front of the TV, with those distant eyes of his, psychotics get that way before an attack, with that look that doesn't focus on anything and seems to be seeing something that you can't see. I said, "Enough, it's over." He went on with those eyes of his, him and his sadness, and never said a single word. I got my things, it may be selfish, I thought, but fuck it, there comes a time when you just have to be selfish. I went to my mother's house. We never saw each other again, or spoke to each other. I don't even know if he's dead or alive. Now, help me clear away these dishes,' she said, getting up from the table.

We spent the rest of the night sitting in the living room, side by side, drinking, listening to music, with me telling myself that I should go, and staying, Melissa is going to call, I said, and stayed, Melissa is by herself, suffering, I thought, and stayed, and there was a moment in which our mouths were so close, our eyes, I'm scum, I thought. The woman I love, suffering, the doctors cutting off the leg of the husband of the woman I love, and me here laughing with a German woman. I got up, thanked her for the dinner, all her help. I was sincere when I told her she was a very interesting woman, and I left before things got complicated.

20

Ronald came home a week later. Melissa would spend the better part of the day at his side. There was little chance for us to see each other; that was the hardest part. Ronald would call for her every three minutes, asking for water, medicine, juice, coffee, newspapers, the remote control, everything had to be handed to him, and immediately, because he was in a terrible mood. He ran the business from his bed, giving orders by phone. The worst part was when it came time for his bath. Melissa had suggested they hire a male nurse, but Ronald didn't want anyone to see his mutilated leg.

She would often call me from a public phone. 'I love you, I needed to say that, I love you, we're going to kill Ronald right away, we're going to kill him however we can,' she said. 'I love you, we'll shoot him, at night,' she said, 'we'll put an end to this.'

The first time we met after Ronald returned home, I felt sorry for her. Melissa had lost a lot of weight, she was pale, and had dark circles under her eyes. I was forced to make her even more unhappy, by lying and saying that our boa had died. 'Things are going to get better,' she said. 'Life can't be a total piece of shit like this.' When we took off our clothes, life got better immediately. She told me the only thing that mattered to her was our love, 'and my ophidians,' she said. 'I adore you and my ophidians, that's all that matters, the snakes and you. The rest can go to hell.'

'Then come away with me,' I said. 'Leave Ronald and move in here. I'm not afraid of Ronald, we'll confront the guy.'

'Don't you want to kill him?'

'It's not necessary to kill him anymore.'

'No, you're wrong. We have to kill him, we have to go all the way.'

'No,' I said, 'Ronald's nothing now. He won't stand in the way of what we decide to do. He has no power. The accident finished him. Think about it, just who is Ronald anyway? He's a cripple.'

'You don't understand,' she said. 'One day, when I'm walking down the street, coming out of a movie, shopping, I'll be shot three times in the back. It'll happen. He threatens me every day. It'll happen. We have to kill him.'

Melissa had it all thought out. We would kill Ronald by imitating the plot of my book *The Sun Alone.* We would take Ronald to their beach house in Ubatuba. In the morning, she would put him on a sailboat, already half out of it from the sleeping pills she would put in his milk. Ronald loved sailing. I'd rent a boat and meet them on the high seas. We'd hit him a couple of times with the oars, just to knock him out, and throw the body in the water. A few hours later she would contact the Coast Guard and tell them her husband had gone sailing and hadn't returned.

'A cripple doesn't go sailing by himself,' I said.

'It depends on the cripple,' she said. 'A happy cripple, no. But a depressed cripple, one who's contemplating suicide . . .'

'It won't work.'

'You want to give up.'

'It's not that; he's crippled.'

Melissa sat on my bed. 'He's not totally crippled,' she said. 'Ronald can walk with crutches. Have you seen these bruises on my leg? They're from him hitting me with his crutches.'

'I'm not a writer,' I said. '*The Sun Alone* is *The Talented Mr Ripley*, by Patricia Highsmith.'

I took Melissa to the bookcase and showed her all the books I had copied, or tried to copy, while I was working at Minnesota Publishing. *The Stranger*, by Camus; 'The Black Cat', by Edgar Allan Poe; *Double Indemnity*, by James Cain; 'The Man in the Passage', by Chesterton; *Crime and Punishment*, by Dostoevsky; *The Murder of Roger Ackroyd*, by Agatha Christie; *Bufo & Spallanzani*, by Rubem Fonseca; 'The Murders in the Rue Morgue', by Poe; *The Human Beast*, by Zola.

'*A Train to Death* isn't yours?' she asked.

'It's *Double Indemnity*,' I replied, 'by James Cain. The one you're holding in your hand.'

She leafed through it. 'You copied all this? You didn't make up those crimes? I thought you were a specialist in such things.'

'In killing husbands?'

She heard what I said but pretended she hadn't. She sat on the bed and avoided looking at me. That was when the phone rang. The answering machine picked up and a female voice came through, someone named Alice, saying that she'd bought my boa and that the people at the store had given her my number. She needed advice. 'Please call me,' she said, '8742–6671.'

Melissa got up, without looking at me. 'You sold our boa,' she said, 'you bastard.' She picked up her purse, determined.

I felt that things were about to explode. Take control, I thought, take control of the situation, it's easy. 'You're looking for a pretext,' I said, 'a pretext to bail out.' I blocked the door.

'Get out of my way,' she said.

'I'm no good to you anymore,' I said. 'All I'm good for is killing your husband.'

'Get out of my way,' she repeated.

'I'm not a specialist in these things. Wasn't that how you put it, "these things"? I know very well what you meant by "these things". Killing, you meant killing.'

'Shut up,' she said.

I was as nervous as zebras at the approach of lions. She forced her way past. I didn't push her, I only wanted her to stay; that was when she fell, fell on her own, I didn't push anybody, I dropped down beside her, begged her forgiveness, but it was as if she were made of stone. She got up, slammed the door with all her strength, and left. If this had been a film, she would have opened the closet, taken out a suitcase and thrown all her clothes in it, hangers and all. I've never understood why the women in movies always take the hangers when they leave.

21

If I had been searching for a chance to crawl out of the filth, there it was, it couldn't be better. But I wasn't searching for anything. Today, when I look back, I see everything fitting together, forming threads, the threads weaving a story, a terrible story, but at the time I saw nothing. I spent the following days lying down, feeling like a wreck, sinking, having nightmares, yanking the megaphone out of my mother's hands, leaving messages at the vivarium, nothing. Melissa didn't return my calls.

On Wednesday I received a phone call from Mirna asking me to come by Universalis as soon as possible. Until then I hadn't even looked at Pedro Jequitibá's originals. If Laércio got after me about it, I would give him a song-and-dance. I took a shower, picked up a black briefcase so as not to show up empty-handed, and went to the publishing house.

Laércio was unshaven and his round face looked wilted.

'You can stop proofing, Jequitibá just changed publishers,' he said, weary and disheartened. He looked at me, expecting me to say something, but I didn't have anything to say. I listened to the whole story. The night before, Jequitibá had showed up at Laércio's house and flatly announced that he'd signed a nine-hundred-thousand-dollar contract with Mondial, where he would publish the *Learn to* trilogy.

'Didn't you have a contract with him?' I asked.

'Several times he ordered a whole series of clauses changed. Mirna typed and retyped that damned document till she was blue in the face. The truth is that Pedro was already negotiating with Mondial and was playing for time. You can't begin to imagine the things I heard from Pedro on Friday. 'I need a publisher with greater distribution,' he said. He said that Universalis's publicity had never been efficient and that he could have sold three times as many books if he'd published with Mondial. Do you think our distribution is that bad?'

'Yes,' I said.

'OK, but is that any reason to change publishers?'

'You did mention nine hundred thousand dollars.'

'Nine hundred thousand now. Do you know what he was worth when I hired him? Zilch. I made Pedro Jequitibá. He was nothing. I showed him Dale Carnegie's book *How to Win Friends and Influence People* and asked if he could do something along those lines. Pedro practically copied his books, in the beginning. The trilogy itself, the idea for the trilogy, isn't his, it's from another American, I forget the name, I think it's Herbert Richards or something like that. The plagiarist didn't tell me that, but I found out. We were having whiskey at his house, Pedro went to answer the phone, and I was by myself, looking at his bookshelves, when suddenly one title caught my attention. I picked up the book and saw that it was all there, the complete concept for the trilogy. And not just the concept. He copied entire sentences. I had thought that thing he said about "an easy and pleasant way to say no" was really hot shit. It's not his. It's the American's. I also found in the American's book another chapter that spoke about humiliation. Pedro stole that too. Pedro is a repugnant plagiarist.'

Laércio sat at his desk, discouraged.

'I'm going into bankruptcy.'

'I can write those books for you.'

'The bastard. He copied, I admit that, but he knew what the masses wanted.'

'I know too.'

'No, you don't understand.'

'Everybody wants to be fooled,' I said.

'I'm talking about the kind of writing that's so appealing to so many people.'

'We're talking about the same thing. People like to hear "truths" they already know. And they like to change without budging from where they are. I know how to do that, Laércio.'

'It won't work.'

'Of course it will.'

'A book about what?'

'What do you want it to be about? Tell me and I'll write it. How to ride a bicycle with your child on a sunny Sunday afternoon?'

'Pedagogy doesn't sell.'

'Choose your angel?'

'There are too many angels out there already. No good.'

'How not to make enemies?'

'Our concept is different. Enemies don't matter. If you make friends, you're not going to have enemies. The best thing would be *How to Win Friends and Influence People.* Nobody can do it better than old Dale. Let's face facts.'

'I think *The Instant Manager* is as good as Dale.'

'But José Guber isn't a good name.'

'We could make up an American.'

'Only if we put Ph.D. after his name. Americans have to teach at the University of Stanford, or have a clinic for behavioral studies in Los Angeles. What's your degree in?'

'Journalism.'

Laércio sighed, dispirited.

'I like José Guber,' I said.

'It's not a question of like. It has to work. And there are rules. The first name has to be the name of a saint – Pedro, Tiago, João, in other words, from the animal kingdom. The last name has to be vegetable or mineral, to create a balance between those, those, those – let's call them elements of nature. Agatha, for example, is excellent for a woman. You can call yourself Gonçalo-Alves, which is a hardwood, good for deluxe cabinet-making. Don't like it? Then how about Tiago Argento?'

'I prefer João Peroba.'

'Peroba also means boring. If you don't like Argento, it's because you want to be wood, which is very noble of you. João Aroeira. How about it? It's a medicinal tree.'

'If it's medicinal, that's OK. *Give Yourself a Hand*, that's going to be the title of the book.'

'*Give Yourself a Hand*? Won't people think of –?'

'People like double meanings, especially sexy ones. They've even been legitimized in college curriculums. Think of Shakespeare's "country matters".'

'What's the book about?'

'*Give Yourself a Hand*, the title explains it all. The complete essence of the self-help philosophy is right there. No one can help you if you don't help yourself. If you don't help yourself, God won't help you and neither will anyone else.'

'What else? I like what I'm hearing.'

'I got the idea just now; I have to give it some more thought. That's the concept.'

'*Give Yourself a Hand*. Yeah. We'll do a small printing; all audacity demands a dose of prudence.'

22

We have nothing to fear but words.
– Rubem Fonseca

A few words to begin:
In the lectures I've given around the world, I always mention the case of a gentleman who came to see me at the Universalis Center for Transcendental Counseling. He complained of headaches, nausea, insomnia, and lived in terror of being attacked by some serious disease like cancer or goiter. He was working fourteen hours a day, smoked two packs of cigarettes, ate anything that was set before him, and spent his nights in front of the television, watching war movies 'to relax'. His doctor had already done the diagnosis – stress – and recommended a vacation, but he always refused to obey because when he took a vacation it created expectations. He felt that he had to rest, sleep, exercise. He would rent a house at the beach, spend a fortune getting everything ready, driving hundreds and hundreds of miles, and when he got to the place he didn't feel the slightest pleasure. He would get irritated at the sand, at the sun, at the house, wouldn't exercise, would put on weight, sleep badly, and, worst of all, he couldn't stop thinking about work. Things being as they were, he preferred not to take a

vacation. When I asked him what he thought the cause of such torment was, he replied that he had an enemy. Someone who told him, 'You're insignificant, you're a failure, you're fat, you only think about eating, you do everything wrong, you don't go anywhere, don't try, don't start, don't finish, leave everything half done.' 'If that's the case,' I said, 'the first thing to do is cut off all contact with that negative individual, that person who sends you nothing but destructive messages.' 'How can I cut off myself?' he answered. 'I'm my enemy. I'm the one doing it to me.'

I suppose you're thinking that this was a case of some eccentric, some obsessive neurotic. Right? You're mistaken. He was a perfectly normal guy. And there's more. Large numbers of people with problems similar to his show up at our center.

But, let's get to the point. When we examine what holds us back from achieving happiness, love, friends, self-confidence, professional success, we come to this conclusion: it's someone else's fault. It's your boss, it's your husband, it's your wife, it's the country, it's the economy, and so forth. However, according to latest research from the American group Science of Biochemical Behavior, 94 per cent of failures are themselves the cause of their failures. And how do we fail? The same way as that gentleman who sought me out. With our mouths. Our words.

This book will teach you how to change your life through transformation of your vocabulary. You will learn how to use the right word at the right time to the right person, and thus progress in your professional, financial, and emotional life. You will learn to look at yourself in the mirror and say, 'Today is going to be a beautiful day, even if it rains,' and in so doing change your reality for the better. Let's get down to work.

P. S. Laércio, as you can see, there are some 'incorrectnesses' in the introduction, like for example my lectures, the Universalis Center for Transcendental Counseling, but as you suggested, I studied the American introductions, and the empirical question is fundamental. If we don't have the Ph.D., if we don't have Stanford, if we don't have a clinic in California, the only thing left is to fantasize a little. In short, we have to take a chance. If the book works out, we can open the Center and make up the lectures. If it doesn't work out, who's going to care about our untruths?

The idea for the *Give Yourself a Hand* book was very simple. You can only help yourself by doing the right thing. And to do the right thing you have to say the right thing. That's why I've created my symbiotic vocabulary, a proposal for behavior modification based on constructive language. Words and you, your body, your mind, your spirit, everything interacts symbiotically. From changing your vocabulary, your whole life will change. Euphemisms and metaphors are good for the health, I said in my book. Euphemism is the use of a happy and positive word instead of an unhappy and negative one. And metaphor is when you say things in an indirect way. For example, don't say, 'My romance with that wonderful woman is over.' Say, 'The crisis is temporary.' Say, 'She'll come back.' Say, 'She's going to phone me.' Say, 'I'll do whatever she wants.' Domesticate words as you would a wild pig; that was the first lesson in my book. Expunge from your vocabulary words like fear, failure, jealousy, anguish. They contaminate your system like a tainted oyster.

I was working diligently on my book when the phone rang. I answered. It was a man's voice. 'This is Ronald Amarante,' he said. 'We met in the country, at the hotel in São Francisco. I'm calling to thank you. My wife told me you were a great help to us. I'd like to invite you to dinner at my house this weekend.'

It was the opportunity I thought I needed. I accepted. We set it for Saturday at eight.

23

We were in Ronald's living room, he, Melissa, and me, each of us with a whiskey glass in our hands; I was on my second round. A very comfortable house, uncluttered, one of those you see in the rich area of the southern coast, with exposed brickwork. It was devilishly hot, Melissa didn't look at me, didn't open her mouth; I didn't say anything either. As a matter of fact, that was one of the rules I had incorporated into my symbiotic vocabulary. Let the human being talk, all that the human being longs for is a pair of ears to serve as outlet for his problems and gripes. I had copied that from Pedro Jequitibá, and judging by what Laércio had told me, it was no problem. 'People copy from others,' he said. 'You copy from Jequitibá, Jequitibá copies from the Americans, the Americans copy from the Indians. There's no end to the borrowing.' Silence, I said in my book, is a form of dialogue. If in doubt, keep quiet. Listen.

'In the intensive care unit,' Ronald said, 'I had the impression that I was dead. Everything white, moans, I'm dead, I thought. One day, when I was less doped up, I saw a woman, a lady in white, closely resembling a deceased aunt of mine, who told me we were in the hospital. The ICU taught me one thing: doctors have the souls of dogs. They're a wretched race of people. They're worse than politicians, than lawyers, than accountants. I hate doctors. They jammed tubes up me, stuck needles in me, and the whole time talking about how unreliable cell phones are. When the doctor told me, "We're going to have to amputate your leg," I felt like saying, "OK then, you're fired." As if he were a plywood wholesaler that I could replace with another one, but in medicine you can't replace anybody. Each one is worse than the next. More whiskey?'

Ronald talked nonstop. I asked, though I don't know just why, maybe because I was drunk, if he believed in God and he answered that he believed in God but not in science. 'A snakebite,' he said, 'and I lose a leg.'

'What are legs for?' I asked.

'To walk with,' he said.

'Yes, to walk with. Fine, I have two legs. Does that make me any better than you? A donkey has four legs, a table has four legs, three more than you.'

I think I'd had too much to drink. I noticed that Ronald and Melissa were looking at me, puzzled.

'I'm going to wear a mechanical leg, I mean, electronic leg, or something like that,' Ronald said. 'It seems they've made a lot of progress in that area.'

During dinner, which by the way was magnificent, Ronald became even more depressed. Melissa ignored me completely, constantly looking at Ronald, want some more, dear, more this, more that? Why was she treating him so delicately? The cripple refused everything, sat there staring at the plate with those dog's eyes of his, smiling an idiotic smile, unhappy, now the dog was unhappy, that on top of everything else, since he'd lost a leg he was more humble, sad, maybe he didn't even beat his wife anymore. And she, from what I saw, was enjoying not being beaten by the gimp.

Maybe the two of them had had a talk and set things straight, I won't beat you anymore, he must have said, let's go to Paris, start over again, people with money can go to Paris to start over again, I thought, yes, she must have answered, let's have a baby, it's times like that when the babies come along, they break the vessel of marriage and try to glue it back together with babies, in Paris, sometimes it's that way, I'll bet that's how it was, they had come to an understanding, they'd have a baby, go to Paris, and there I was, the fifth wheel, wasting my time. I suffered at that dinner. Melissa was nothing but smiles and courtesies with her husband, and that made me suffer. If Melissa isn't playacting, I thought, if she's really smiling at her husband, if she doesn't want anything more to do with me, I thought, I'm finished. What was there in my life besides Melissa? Nothing. The truth is that I had never been in love. Before Melissa I would take women to bed and think only about fucking and leaving, going home, I didn't want any woman in my apartment, in the bed where I slept every day, I wanted to fuck and that was all, and when I got home I couldn't even remember what the woman's breasts were like or the precise color of her hair, or what her smell was like, but with Melissa it was different, I knew what her navel was like, and her big toe, and I took her to my apartment and let her fill my sheets with the smell of her, I wanted to be with her all day long, making love and talking to her, even if it was about snakes or murder.

After dinner, while Melissa was clearing the table, I asked to go to the bathroom and waited in the hall. When she came by with the trays, I pulled her inside the powder room. 'Be careful,' she said. I put the dishes on the toilet, seated her on the washbasin, kissed her face. 'Stop,' she said. I didn't stop. 'You're a coward,' she said. I raised her skirt. 'Coward.' I pulled her panties aside. 'Coward,' she repeated over and over. While we fucked, I whispered in her ear that I hadn't sold our boa constrictor; someone had turned me in, I said, some son of a bitch, I said, I'd received a phone call from the environmental agency, I said, and had taken the snake to a store belonging to friends, they had sold it without my authorization, I said, those sons of bitches, I said, while she came. I didn't come. I kneeled and stuck my face between her legs, told her that I was a slave, I'll kill that basket case, I said, I'll kill him right now if you want me to.

24

Words are useless.
– James Joyce

Or very useful. It depends on you.

This is the situation. It's hot. You've had a horrible day. Your boss was in a bad mood and argued with you. It was unpleasant; your idiot of a boss said some really unpleasant things. You get home and the children are fighting over a new toy their grandmother brought from Miami. And your wife looks peeved. What do you do? Do you dump your bag of garbage on them, complaining and slamming doors? There's another alternative. Take off your coat and say how good it is to be home, say kind words about how nice dinner smells, relate a funny event that occurred during the day, or tell a joke. Sit on the floor with the kids, say good, educational things. Do this and I guarantee you a pleasant evening.

In this chapter I suggest that you do a diagnostic of your vocabulary.

Tell me the words you use and I'll tell you what your quality of life is and the outlook for your future.

Write down on a sheet of paper the words you use when:

1. Your wife (or husband) criticizes you.
2. Your friend is half an hour late for lunch/dinner.

3. Another driver cuts you off in traffic. (Or when you're stuck in a traffic jam.)
4. The attendant at the bank (or any public office) is slow.
5. The guy in front of you at the ATM doesn't know how to work it.
6. You want to wear a certain shirt and the maid (or your wife) hasn't washed it, though it's Monday and she's had all weekend to do it.
7. There's a rumor that the company is going to downsize.
8. Someone is hired with an exemplary résumé.
9. You've got the flu and someone asks how you feel.
10. You can't do the task your boss has assigned you.
11. A neighbor you don't like gets into the elevator with you.
12. Tickets for the next show at the movies run out just as you get to the ticket booth.

Melissa with no clothes on, a book in her hands. We were lying in my bed. 'The tongue licks,' I was reading the poem aloud, 'the tongue licks the red petals –'

'Stop reading poetry and let's get back to work,' Melissa said, taking the book out of my hand.

'Then put on your clothes,' I said, 'your legs destroy my ability to think. This is the most I can read with you naked beside me.' Melissa got between the covers.

'Take a look at this,' she said, handing me a different book, full of red underlining. Another crime. That was our routine.

I knew what we would find in the detective novels. Gunshots, stabbings, and poison were the most common means of killing, and each of these modalities allowed countless variations. It could also be strangulation, a blow to the temporal lobes or the base of the skull, defenestration, asphyxia with a pillow or plastic bag, electrocution, gasoline-soaked clothing set on fire, drowning in the bathtub, it could be whatever we wanted. We studied very hard, Melissa and I. We burrowed into those books the way worms burrow into dead bodies, Christie, Sayers, Chandler, Hammett, Doyle, Hillerman, Block, Stout, Simenon, Marsh, Collins, Dickson Carr, Westlake, Conrad, Rendell, Spillane, Dostoevsky, Bentley, Dickens, Eco, Chesterton, Stocker – name an author and we read him. We made several lists, the way those American publications do, ideal places to hide a body, the best weapon, appropriate places to commit a crime, feasibility, and style. We thought about faking an accident, throwing Ronald from a train like in *Double Indemnity*, our favorite. We thought about killing him with a bullet in the head and leaving him in the trunk of a car rented in his name at the airport, like in *Prizzi's Honor.* We thought about everything. In reality there are a thousand ways to kill somebody, even if the victim takes precautions such as having someone taste his food. They say that Ferdinand de' Medici eliminated his brother in a very ingenious way. He poisoned only one of the sides of a knife blade, picked up a peach, cut it in half, gave the poisoned half to his brother, and calmly ate the other half.

The time we spent in bed, reading and making love, jotting down ideas and discussing our literary research, did us absolutely no good. We would find something, this could be useful, we would say, excited, finally a good killing, and then give up a few pages later when we ran into a detail whose adaptation to our project was very difficult if not downright impossible.

There's no such thing as the perfect crime. There's not a single detective novel that offers a true perfect crime. There are artistic, highly original, very cerebral crimes, and there's a lot of stupidity all around us. There are many shortcomings in the investigations, but you can't count on that when you're planning to kill someone, because there's also happenstance, you have to consider, there are intelligent detectives, there are witnesses, there's everything. What should be considered is the place, the opportunity, that was the only thing the books taught me. You should know the victim like the back of your hand and the scene of the crime too. Know in detail everything that goes on there, the people who frequent the location.

All this was discussed diligently. And so, finally, our plan emerged.

25

I have to admit that I was never the brave type. Therefore it was natural that, even with Melissa at my side, encouraging me and giving me reasons for killing Ronald, I was afraid. So afraid that I spent night after night awake, thinking about the crime and its consequences, and when I would fall asleep it was a restless sleep with horrible nightmares.

What helped me at this dark moment of my life, besides Melissa of course, was my symbiotic vocabulary. It's important to state that until I was hired by Universalis I had never read self-help books; it wasn't prejudice, just simple lack of interest in the subject matter.

But, one day, I was at a meeting at the publisher's, discussing the symbiotic vocabulary with Laércio, when a man appeared and asked to speak to the author of *Learn to Love Yourself.* I said that Jequitibá wasn't there; what was it he wanted to talk about? The guy answered, 'I want to kiss that man's hands. He saved my life. Really, I'm not exaggerating.' And the guy told me how Jequitibá had saved his life. He didn't have the money to buy the things he needed, his private life wasn't going well, his professional life was even worse, and nobody, *nobody* helped him. While *others* progressed in life, receiving considerations and being favored with every type of advantage, he received nothing, not even his due. He was a broken man, embittered, envious and unhappy, who blamed others for his misfortunes and who harbored, in his own words, 'only hate and despair in my heart'. He thought about ending his miserable life, after killing his two-year-old son 'to spare him from living in this world full of injustice'. The words are his. One day he was walking dejectedly down the street after leaving his office early, thinking of killing himself that night, when he saw *Learn to Love Yourself* in the window of a bookstore. Without knowing why, he went in and bought the book. And also without knowing why, when he got home he started reading it. He read it in one sitting. When he finished, without knowing why, he decided to follow 'the precepts of the book', in his words, and in a short time his life changed, he began to have a better relationship with his wife, his relatives, and his fellow workers, he was promoted, and now he's a happy, fulfilled man, all because he learned, the words are his, 'that the first thing a man must do is love himself'.

And the most interesting part is that, as that man was talking, I was thinking: It's true, that's what's happening to me. My symbiotic vocabulary was giving me the strength for anything. My new attitude, my clarity of reasoning, my disposition, my correct words, my way of speaking – I was changing, and it had to do with my new vocabulary. I changed. For example, I came to no longer tolerate my mother's excesses. I yanked the megaphone from her hands and threw it out. She went out of her head and I didn't let it get to me, as I normally would have. And when she started yelling from the window and the neighbors came to me with a petition, I didn't hesitate; I put my mother in a rest home. She would hardly speak to me at first; she would turn her head when I went to visit her. Earlier, that would have killed me. But I repeated to myself, I'm the way I am. I think the way I think. I want this for me. I planned the details of Ronald's murder, and felt that I wouldn't back out; I would go ahead. I'm going ahead, I repeated to myself. That was proof of the power of the good word. Books shouldn't be written only to amuse, as I used to do, but to teach, edify, and save.

Beyond the technical preparation, Melissa and I trained emotionally, using my subliminal exercises which, as I observed, created a stimulus that acted in the deepest layers of consciousness.

Melissa was very good in these rehearsals. She was the first to test my exercises.

26

Subliminal exercises

Circles: Draw a large circle on a piece of paper. Tape it to the wall. Close your eyes and try to put your finger in the center of the circle.

One: One is the magic number. It is the beginning of everything, the first rung on the ladder leading you to success. Use the word one a lot. Inhale. In exhaling, say wuuuuuuuuuunnnn, filling the recesses of your face with the sound so that the whole of your cheeks trembles. Repeat the exercise five times.

Revelatory exercises

I: *I* is the word human beings use most. Whenever someone says anything, the word *I* appears. Feel the I that you're saying. Stand before a mirror, look at your face and say, I, I-I-I-I-I-I-I-I-I-I-I, thinking about the I that is you. And later, when it appears, in any form, think about what the I is doing in the middle of your words.

Let's get to the facts. At Melissa's suggestion, Ronald phoned me again on a Thursday afternoon, his voice animated, to tell me he had started using the mechanical leg and inviting me to have a whiskey with him.

I got there ten minutes early. There was something wrong with the outside intercom, which meant the maid had to open the gate in person. That was very good. I jotted down in my notebook: don't get the intercom fixed.

As I had asked, Melissa delayed a few minutes before coming downstairs with Ronald. I wandered aimlessly around the house, seeing where the telephones were in the living room, the garden, the access to the living-room door, the access to the rear entrance, I played the nosy guest and went to the kitchen to ask for water, claiming I had to take a pill. I saw the pantry, just as Melissa had described it, the back door, the rear wall that separated the house from the neighbors. On my way back to the living room I made a sketch on a sheet of paper.

Ronald came down first. The mechanical leg was a real success. You could hardly tell. He even took off his shoe to show me. Even the material was incredible; it imitated skin, toes, in very impressive fashion.

But what impressed me most was Ronald himself. A correct, genteel man, well dressed, the type of fellow you look at and say, 'That's one cool guy.' Melissa had told me his entire story, from the time he was an insignificant little businessman, owner of a construction-supply store, a small shed stuffed with ropes, tools, sacks of cement and whitewash. Ronald had hired Melissa as a seller, and three months later they got married. They were happy at first. Melissa got admitted to the university, studied biology, while Ronald opened a second store and then a third. The business was going well, but he had already begun calling her silly and stupid and a cow. Later, when Melissa began working, Ronald started beating her. 'There are men,' Melissa said, 'who only feel pleasure when they're hitting their wives.'

After she met me, things got even worse. Melissa told me that when she asked Ronald for a separation his response was to break her arm.

I looked at Ronald and tried to see the man crazy about money, violent, aggressive, a wife-beater, a man who locked his wife in her room on a bright Sunday just to see her suffer, but the person before me was a husband out of a margarine commercial.

Ronald made a whiskey for me and one for himself, and afterwards, when Melissa joined us, as beautiful as always, we had a couple more rounds. At dinner we drank two more bottles of wine.

I was on the alert for everything, noting all the details.

When I was thinking of leaving, Ronald asked me to wait; he wanted to show Melissa and me something. He went to the stereo, put on a CD. 'Watch this,' he said.

Ronald began to tap dance. He moved from side to side in the room, his legs out of control; several times I almost went to grab him, thinking he was about to fall. At the end he made the classic gesture of appreciation, bowing his head and spreading his arms. He asked if we had liked it. I said yes; Melissa didn't answer.

I went home wanting to chuck the whole thing. If I hadn't seen the marks on Melissa's body the next day, from the punches and kicks, it's quite likely I would have chucked it.

27

Cover layout

Do you want success? Money? Do you want to change your life? If so, *Give Yourself a Hand.*

(Laércio, this is the text that should appear in large type on the cover.) Below, in red, comes the title *Give Yourself a Hand.* The cover is blue, with the drawing of a hand, palm up, the symbol of asking and offering. My pseudonym appears in red. João Aroeira. *Learning to Help Yourself.*

Underneath is an attractive photo of a strong-looking man with his hand on his chin, smiling. I thought about using this photo of my brother Moisés, which is enclosed. Moisés was a tremendous success with women when he was alive. What do you think?

On the back cover, more text: João Aroeira, thirty-five, who introduced the teaching of the techniques of behavioral modification through symbiotic linguistics.

It was a dirt road, very narrow, a real washboard. There wasn't a living soul in the vicinity. Ahead of us were disused oil wells. I parked next to the platform, we got out of the car. A strong wind, she kept fixing her hair in the side mirror of my Chevrolet. I went to the well; I wanted to see the pump house. It was full of junk and appeared to have been deactivated long ago. I walked toward the Chevrolet. She was standing outside. 'Gimme the gun,' she said. I placed the gun in her hand and picked up a can from the ground.

'I'm going to put this can over there,' I said, pointing to an abandoned car. 'Don't shoot till I give the OK, understand?' She spit out her gum.

'OK, all I gotta do is pull the trigger?'

I turned around and set the can on the hood of the automobile. As I was returning, she pointed the revolver at my chest. 'Stop right there, you son of a bitch.' I heard a sharp crack but didn't even consider stopping. She fired twice more.

I woke up and expelled James Cain from my head. No, not James Cain. Chandler, *The Big Sleep*. Lately I'd been dreaming of nothing but the crimes I'd researched. It was torture.

When you've got a dirty job to do, draw up a plan and carry it out at once, that's my advice. Otherwise, it'll be in the foreground, the plan, provoking nightmares every night, getting in the way of your perspective, your reasoning, forming swamps, and what you used to think was really good stops being so good, doubts arise, you become insecure, think you're going to get caught. I was fed up with that. I called Melissa at work and told her it would be that night.

The basic virtue of our plan was its simplicity. We would do what everybody thinks of doing. I suggested it myself, and it was my symbiotic vocabulary that brought it to my attention. At the time, we were doing our literary research and I said, 'We're after something original, but what we really need is the old hands-up approach, that's how you kill people in Brazil.' I got a few clippings from old newspapers and showed Melissa the numbers. 'The days are gone when heart attacks were the major cause of death in São Paulo,' I said. 'The number of people who die in robberies is much higher than those who die from myocardial infarction. Just look at the statistics. It'll be easy. You leave the kitchen door unlocked, I come in and take care of the matter in two minutes.'

'You said yourself that the first thing that comes into a woman's head when she thinks about killing her husband is faking a robbery,' Melissa said.

'The problem is that they go about it all wrong. They tell their girlfriends that they have a lover, they send the children to their grandmother's the day of the crime, they tie up the dog that usually runs free, they give the servants the day off. The mistake in a crime such as this is trying to make things easy. We're not going to make anything easy,' I said. 'The door should be locked, the cook doing her cooking, the dog in the yard.'

'The door locked?' Melissa asked. 'Didn't you just say I had to leave the kitchen door unlocked?'

'Yes,' I said. 'I'm speaking in theoretical terms. The police should find the door was locked, but actually you're going to unlock it for me.'

'Ah, good. I thought you were changing the plan.'

'Everything must be proceeding normally, that's what I mean.'

28

Guber,

As we agreed, I'm leaving with your doorman a copy of your book, which I've just picked up at the printer's. I admit that at first I was apprehensive about using your brother's photo on the cover, but I like the result. I think it's going to help sales. Give me a call and tell me how you like it.

Cordially,

Laércio

P. S. Pedro Jequitibá, that lowlife, said in an interview that he'd never read Carnegie. Know what I did? I called the newspaper and told them to compare Chapter 2 of *Learn to Be Happy* with Chapter 6 of *How to Win Friends and Influence People*. Jequitibá mentions the poster he put on the door to his office, You're Important. The plagiarist stole that from Carnegie. Jequitibá even copied verbatim the sentence 'Almost everyone considers himself important. Very important.' In the same chapter, Jequitibá talks about research by the New York Telephone Company that demonstrated that the most frequently used word in phone conversations is the pronoun *I*. That's in Carnegie's book. You used that in an intelligent way in your revelatory exercises. But Jequitibá discussed the matter like an imbecile. And the bum has sold seven hundred thousand copies.

11 p.m. As a precaution, I went around the block on foot. In residential neighborhoods like this one, with short, dark streets, no one is out after eight o'clock unless they're in a car. The sound of television: movies, commercials, newscasts, everybody in front of their TV. The service station was open, but from there, I confirmed, it wasn't possible to get a good view of Melissa's house.

I went back. I jumped the wall, twisting my ankle as I landed. The toy poodle appeared, barking. Its name was Ralph. 'Come here, Ralph,' I said. I broke his neck in the first two minutes. I went through the garden, skirting the house, limping because of my foot; the lights in the living room were on.

I kneeled beside the kitchen door. The sound of water, dishes being washed. I turned the knob, pushed open the door, and went in. When she saw the gun, and the black mask covering my face, the maid recoiled, her eyes wide. She bumped into the table, fell on her back, but made no noise. She saw nothing but my revolver. I took from my coat pocket a roll of duct tape and covered her mouth. Human beings, when they're afraid of dying, are transformed into something disgusting: that moaning, submissive woman was even worse. I felt sorry for her. The poor thing all but peed into her shoes. I took her to the pantry and sat her down in a chair. 'It's all right,' I said. 'Nothing bad is going to happen.' I tied her arms behind her, then her legs, and locked her in.

On my way back, I cut the telephone line. I went down the hall, past the lavatory. Ronald and Melissa were on the sofa, watching TV, when I came in, pointing the gun.

'My God, a robber,' said Melissa. That wasn't in the plan; I found it funny. It was so false on her part that I don't know how Ronald didn't catch it. I went up to them, told Ronald to stand up. He asked me to take it easy, said he would cooperate, that he'd give me money, jewels, the cars, or whatever else I wanted, but please not to do anything to his pregnant young wife, to leave her alone.

'She'll be OK,' I said, and at that moment I saw that Ronald was looking at my eyes, straight into my eyes, I was afraid he had recognized my voice, and I had an awful feeling as if I were about to lose control of the situation. I thought he was going to say something, but Ronald dashed away, heading for the garden. I ran after him, revolver in hand, tripped over the frame of the glass door that led to the garden.

Melissa rushed past me. 'Come on,' she said, 'come on.' It took me a moment to regain my feet. I found Melissa on the porch. 'He's under the car,' she whispered into my ear.

I ran to the garage. There he was, underneath Melissa's car. I bent down and pulled him by the leg, he resisted and the mechanical leg came off in my hand. I grabbed him by the arm and dragged him out. 'Guber?' he said. It wasn't a question. He knew it was me. He wasn't going to scream or struggle. I pointed the gun.

'What are you waiting for?' said Melissa.

'Keep quiet,' I said.

'Shoot,' she said.

I couldn't pull the trigger.

'Go ahead and shoot,' she said. Melissa jerked the revolver from my hand and fired into Ronald's skull. A single shot in the forehead. 'Come on,' she said. 'We don't have any time to waste.'

I followed Melissa, walking slowly. When I got to the kitchen I heard another shot. Melissa came out of the pantry dragging the cook's bloody body by the arms.

'Have you gone mad?' I asked.

'Yes, and don't make me waste any more time. Come on, help me.'

'Goddammit, you killed that poor woman.'

'Goddammit, help me.'

'She never did anything to us.'

'It was just a matter of time,' Melissa said, 'before she opened her mouth. Do you want to take the chance? Come on, careful, she's dripping blood on the runner, move the runner away from there,' she shouted.

We arranged the bodies of Ronald and the cook in the living room and the kitchen. We cleaned up the blood and burned the rags we'd used. We locked the kitchen door and I quickly broke into it the way a thief would. We trashed the rooms, opened drawers, threw things on the floor, broke everything, opened the safe. The jewels and money were put in a small suitcase that Melissa hid in a closet. Last of all, I tied Melissa up in the living room. She wanted me to shoot her in the arm or leg, but I didn't have the nerve. 'Hit me,' she said, already completely bound. I wasn't going to hit her. 'You idiot, do you want to be arrested?' I punched her in the mouth. 'Kick me,' she said. I kicked her. 'Again.' I kicked her again. 'That's enough. I think you broke a tooth.'

I left; no one saw me leave. I threw the gun and the mask in the Tietê River before I went home. The next morning, Laércio called to say they'd sold two thousand five hundred copies of *Give Yourself a Hand.*

Heaven and Hell

. . . And let me speak to the yet unknowing world
How these things came about. So shall you hear
Of carnal, bloody and unnatural acts,
Of accidental judgements, casual slaughters;
Of deaths put on by cunning and forc'd cause;
And, in this upshot, purposes mistook
Fall'n on th' inventors' heads.
All this can I
Truly deliver.

William Shakespeare
Hamlet

29

To: João Aroeira   From: Afonso Moraes,
Sunday Special

As agreed, here are the questions for the interview. Please send them as soon as possible, as the material will be published in this week's *Sunday Special.*

SS: Why such mystery about your personal life?

AROEIRA: There's no mystery at all. It's just that my personal life is nobody's business.

SS: Your photos, which are distributed by Universalis's publicity department, make your women readers sigh. It's natural that they want to know more about you. For example, are you married? What is your routine like? What do you like to do?

AROEIRA: I'm married. I have an absolutely normal life.

SS: Why do you give interviews only by fax?

AROEIRA: I'm much sought-after. Besides my books, I write articles for several magazines and newspapers. I train teams who lecture on the technique of symbiotic equilibrium throughout the country. I'm also setting up a telemarketing center in order better to assist the reader. Therefore I don't have time to receive the press.

SS: Why don't you give your own lectures and courses?

AROEIRA: Because if I did that I'd have to give up writing books.

SS: There are rumors that João Aroeira is the pseudonym of Pedro Jequitibá. What do you say to that?

AROEIRA: Really? The press resents my not addressing them personally. They make up things. The press is very creative.

SS: This last year you published three titles, *Give Yourself a Hand, The Symbiotic Dictionary of Professional Success,* and *The Symbiotic Dictionary of Health,* all of which are on the best-seller list. What do you make of the growth of the self-help market?

AROEIRA: People are searching for their creative energies. I see this quite clearly in the letters I receive. No one says, 'Help me.' They say, 'I want to help myself.' That *I* changes everything. My work proposes exactly that behavioral change, through a basic instrument of expression, which is the word.

SS: You said in an interview that if you were interested in money you'd have chosen a different profession and not be a writer. Do you make money from self-help literature?

AROEIRA: I don't make as much as you people say I do. I work for the enjoyment of it.

SS: Do you yourself follow the suggestions found in your symbiotic vocabularies?

AROEIRA: Generally, when I wake up I do the sequence of basic exercises that is in my first book, Chapter 2. It's an easy sequence, fun to do, and very, very effective. My life changed completely after I created the technique of symbiotic vocabulary. Today I have more energy to work, and greater inclination. I'm more creative and generally achieve my goals.

SS: What will your next book be?

AROEIRA: You're in for a big surprise. That's all I can say.

A round bed, mirrors on the ceiling, clothes everywhere, that was Ingrid's bedroom. She was smoking, naked, her head resting on my chest. I ran my hand lightly along her back, her buttocks two firm spheres that fitted in my hand.

'I was on the plane,' she said, 'with two guys sitting next to me, chatting, talking about women. "Nowadays," one of them said, "you can't hold on to a woman with sex." The guy who wasn't even forty started every sentence with "In my day": in his day, women stayed with good lovers, in his day women were real women, "And now they're citizens, second-class citizens," he said. "That's what feminism did to the modern woman. They've lost their mystery, but they don't care about that because what they want is for men to tell them that women are competent," he said, "even though they've stayed out of philosophy, and out of science for a long time. Before, if you wanted to seduce a woman all you had to do was tell her she was pretty; that doesn't work today, you have to tell her she's competent, rational, practical, and a polyglot." Now here comes the most interesting part. The older, fiftyish one told his friend something like, "The social position of women, machismo, feminism, you name it, all that's pointless when you're talking about the relationship between men and women. Women want men and men want women, that's how things work, normally, of course. I don't know what rejection is," he said, "I've never been rejected by any woman. I've loved women who loved me. If they didn't love me, I wasn't interested. The basic idea of love is receptivity and reciprocity, I open myself and you open yourself and we both enter. I've never understood that business of loving a woman who doesn't want anything to do with you. I've always said from the outset, you have to love me, it's always been that way." I found what the peacock said interesting. The guy, I forgot to mention that the fiftysomething resembled a peacock, the peacock was right, I'm on the peacock's side. Want the good stuff? You have to love me. Do you love me? Or do you just care about fucking, like in the beginning? Answer me,' Ingrid said, pulling me by the hair and kissing me.

'I love you,' I said.

'By my reckoning,' Ingrid said, 'you've loved me since you got rich. It was only after you moved into that tacky house with that crazy blonde. In March. Before that, we would fuck and I would say, "I love you," and you would say, "I adore fucking you." The week you moved there, I said, "I love you," and you answered, "I love you too."'

I got up, began putting on my clothes. 'Where are you going?' Ingrid asked. 'Have dinner with me, I'll make pumpkin purée for you.'

I explained to her that I couldn't. Melissa had asked me to have dinner at home.

'If you've already explained to that Lucrezia Borgia that you're getting a separation, why do you have to have dinner with her?'

I didn't like it when Ingrid referred to Melissa in that manner. I was still very much tied to Melissa, we were still together, Melissa and I. It wasn't love, obviously; after the marriage everything changed, it wasn't love, or sex, it was a bond of a different kind, more handcuffs than bond. Things began coming apart; first we began not to find things enjoyable, and we went on to measuring our words, then we lost that insane desire to go to bed, and routine set in, there remained only a vestige of affection, a vestige, respect, routine, nothing more. A corpse weighs heavily on your back. But I liked Melissa, really and truly liked her, cared about her.

'Your snake-raising wife,' Ingrid said, 'needs to know that you're in the process of getting a separation, and when couples separate they don't have dinner together. He has dinner with his girlfriend, his lover, who will soon take over the throne, and his ex can just look out for herself. She can have dinner with her snakes. Doesn't she like snakes?'

'Yes,' I said, 'and so do I; snakes are very interesting.'

'I hate snakes and crocodiles,' Ingrid answered. 'I hate anything that crawls. Know what Mirna told me? Your wife called me a Teutonic cow. Lucrezia isn't very creative. I'm the equine type. She could have called me a Teutonic mare.'

I kissed Ingrid, she pulled me to the bed again, climbed on top of me, saying, 'Your Teutonic mare has something to show you.'

30

São Paulo, January 22. Peaceful Refuge. Saturday.
José, you ungrateful child, today I send you St James, controlling one's tongue: 'And the tongue is a fire, a world of iniquity. So is the tongue among our members, that it defileth the whole body, and setteth on fire the course of nature; and it is set on fire of hell. For every kind of beasts, and of birds, and of serpents, and of things in the sea, is tamed, and hath been tamed of mankind. But the tongue can no man tame; it is an unruly evil, full of deadly poison.'

Be well. From the mother who adores you, Rosário de Deus.

Sitting at the head of the table, I noticed the perfect placement of the silverware. The white tablecloth, napkins, glasses for water and wine, vases decorated with flowers, and me there, waiting for the delicacies, totally without appetite. 'What are you thinking?' Melissa asked, coming into the dining room carrying a tray with two steaming platters and a salad.

'Nothing,' I said. 'Silliness.'

'You're unhappy,' she said. 'I know it.'

We ate in silence. Melissa ate only the salad.

The telephone rang three times and stopped, before

Melissa could reach it. It was Ingrid's code; she always did that. I had asked Ingrid a million times not to call my house unless it was necessary; I didn't want to cause Melissa pain. People don't understand a relationship that ends without the traditional mudslinging, fights, name-calling, confusion. Ingrid liked to think she was the reason behind the end of my marriage. But the truth is there was no reason; my marriage simply came to an end, and the saddest part is that it became merely a business, bills to pay, social functions, dear, pass the rice, a healthy business in which the partners, care for some salad?, in which despite their differences the partners, you've eaten so little, despite their differences the partners, my stomach is still giving me trouble, despite their differences the partners, it's stress, too much work, despite their differences the partners sit down at the table and converse amicably. When you get married, you think that won't happen with you. But it does. Time passes and the day arrives when you're beside that woman, at the table, in the living room, in bed, anywhere, and you realize it's over. At first you force yourself, you feel sorry, sorry for yourself, for the woman, what the devil is happening? It ends; it's pure shit when it happens, but love ends. You killed a guy because of her, you put your mother in a nursing home so you could be with her, you made money and built the house she wanted to live in; none of that's going to make any difference. Love ends just the same. And Melissa, I recognized, wasn't asking much of me. She could ask for the house, that was her right, 50 per cent of everything I had earned with my books. But she had acted correctly. She asked only that we stay together until the inquiry into Ronald's death was closed, which according to our lawyer was about to happen. Why the hell couldn't Ingrid understand that?

I got up from the table and answered the phone on the first ring. Ingrid always said I had the voice of an encyclopedia salesman when Melissa was in the room. 'The meeting with Laércio is tomorrow at ten,' she said.

'I know, you already told me.'

'Is that so?' she said, imitating my tone of voice. 'I already told you. I know. Then the gentleman should be prepared. That shark Laércio is kind of wary. He senses that we're preparing to pounce.'

'Uh-huh,' I said.

'I hate that plastic way you talk,' she said. 'Uh-huh my ass, and stop calling me Dona Ingrid. I prefer Teutonic cow. Go have dinner with your sweet little wifey.' Click.

'Yes, thank you very much, Dona Ingrid.' I returned to the table.

'Is it because of her we're getting separated?' Melissa asked. I tried to repeat my speech from the night before, saying that such suspicion was unfounded and absurd, totally absurd.

'Ingrid, Dona Ingrid, is a serious young woman. People are very shallow, they say things, they make things up –'

Melissa interrupted me. 'My problem,' she said, 'is that I'm smart. No one has to tell me anything. I feel it, I know it. You're having an affair with Ingrid and that's all there is to it.'

After dinner, the maid brought us coffee in the library. Melissa sat down beside me, carrying a snake coiled around her arm, an albino Indian python, and insisted I hold it. 'It's a rare specimen,' she said. 'It cost a thousand dollars.' I let her put the python in my lap. 'Does she know about

Ronald?' Melissa asked. The snake crawled slowly up my arm, wrapping itself quickly around my neck. 'Does she know about Ronald?'

I felt a strong pressure around my neck. I asked Melissa to help me. 'Does she know about Ronald?'

'Quick,' I said.

'Don't make any sudden movements,' she said. 'You might frighten it.'

'Get it off me,' I said, 'hurry.'

'Are you afraid?'

'Get it off.'

'It sees you're afraid.'

'Get it off.'

Deftly, Melissa made the serpent slide down her arm. 'It's been fed. It would never attack.' I felt a flush course through my body.

Melissa tried to talk about our marriage, suggesting that we go somewhere. 'Maybe Paris,' she said. 'Maybe someplace far away from here, far away from Ingrid . . .'

I replied that there was no point in resuming that discussion.

'There's no more love between us, you told me so yesterday. But there is a corpse, and when it comes to uniting two people, a corpse works as well or better than passion itself.'

I felt terrible anxiety. I went to the bathroom and vomited. I gargled with mouthwash and rinsed my face. When I returned, Melissa wasn't there. I went to my room; we slept in separate bedrooms. Read a bit. Before going to sleep, I noticed the light in Melissa's room was on. I went in. When I approached to pull the cover over her, I saw she was clutching something to her chest. It was Ronald's mechanical leg.

I returned to my room. I got between the covers and turned off the light.

I awoke the next day feeling a burning in the upper part of my stomach, along with a headache. I opened the drawer of the night table and took out a blister card of antacids and chewed two tablets.

I got up. Melissa had gone to the country estate, they told me. Two months after Ronald's death Melissa had sold the stores, bought a place in the country, and begun devoting herself to the illegal trade in poisonous species and the smuggling abroad of refined venom from various snakes such as *jararacas* and rattlesnakes.

I showered, got dressed; I wasn't feeling well. I was sweating profusely. I sat in the garden, loosened my tie. The pool boy was removing leaves from it with a long-handled scoop. He smiled at me. The nausea returned. I went to the bathroom but couldn't vomit.

31

João Aroeira's book still heads best-seller index
João Aroeira stays atop the list with *The Symbiotic Dictionary of Health. Give Yourself a Hand,* his first book, the leading seller throughout the first half of the year, returned to the best-seller list and occupies fourth place, for the third consecutive week.

I put the newspaper that Laércio had given me on the desk. He looked at me with satisfaction, smiling with his stained teeth. 'Do you pray?' I asked. He told me he only remembered God 'when things get rough'.

I showed him an American magazine with a poll about religion. Fifty-one per cent of Americans pray, according to research. And if God doesn't answer, no problem; they go on praying, that's what the research says. The reasons were listed there, sickness, unemployment, disillusionment, infertility, drug dependency, abandonment, everything.

Laércio glanced at the magazine, uninterested. 'So what?' he asked. 'We work a different side of the street. What do you want with this?' I explained that the Catholic Church in Brazil was losing 600,000 followers a year and that cults were proliferating.

'Seems normal enough to me,' he said, trying to get off

the subject. 'People are looking for peace and comfort. It's that simple.'

'Yes, that's precisely the issue. You've put your finger on it. Please, have a seat.'

'You really want to talk about this?' Laércio asked.

'Yes, I do.' Laércio sat down. I sensed his impatience growing uncontrollably. 'You hit the nail on the head. The key word is *comfort.* People want peace, comfort, and the Church doesn't give comfort to anyone.'

'I understand,' he said, looking at his watch.

'These days the Church is neither fish nor fowl, it's there like a grazing cow, and now and then it opens its mouth to say it's against abortion. Take a look at these numbers.'

'I know,' Laércio said.

'Every year,' I continued, 'thousands of people disappear from their homes in various countries around the world and enter those crazy cults. There was one year when nine hundred people in one of those cults died after taking cyanide.'

'I thought this meeting was to talk about your next book,' Laércio said, in a tone that irritated me.

'We're going to talk to these people,' I said. 'We're going to write books for them. We're going to teach them how to pray. I want to write about God in a constructive way. I want to propose a peaceful, healthy relationship with God. And I want to use my own name. Enough of pseudonyms.'

Laércio looked at me, agonized. He didn't reply for several moments. 'You don't simply abandon a success like João Aroeira,' he said finally. 'João Aroeira isn't just a name any longer, it's a trademark. Do you think if the books had José Guber's name on them we'd sell a million and a half copies? Guber is a German name. It's fine for beer. I understand your point of view. Everybody talks about João Aroeira and José Guber is an unknown, a nobody. It's hard to listen to praise in silence. We feel like shouting, I know that. We shouldn't have put Moisés's photo on the covers. That was your idea, you recall, but what's done is done. If it's any help to you, let me tell you, success is shit. I'm a publisher, I know the human soul. You have all this comfort and live a peaceful life. Your neighbors aren't hounding you for autographs. Do you know what it's like not to be able to go to a drugstore for condoms without being recognized?'

'There are several reasons for you to change your mind,' I said. 'One is that the evangelic publishers are exploding.'

'Self-help sells more,' he said, 'I know the market.'

'The other reason,' I said, 'is me. I want to write about God. I'll do it with you, if you want to. Naturally I'm not talking just about good advances or a straight 10 per cent royalty. I'm talking about shares in Universalis, about a partnership. But you might not want it, I know that, and in that case I can roll up my sleeves and do the book on my own. I'll open up a publishing house and that'll be it. But I don't want to seem like I'm taking advantage. The choice is yours,' I said.

It was a hard blow for Laércio. He stammered, paced in circles, coughed, and when he left my office I saw he was completely disoriented.

Ingrid came into my office immediately afterwards. 'The shark had an ugly expression on his face,' she said. 'How did the conversation go?'

'There wasn't any conversation,' I said. 'I dumped it all on him, he stood there staring at me with that sour look on his face and said he'd think about it.'

'Think about what? Didn't he understand? Did you tell

him? We change publishers. We can sell to Catholics, Pentecostals, evangelicals . . .'

I sat down on the sofa and asked for some water. Ingrid opened a bottle of mineral water, gave it to me, and sat down beside me. 'You look green,' she said. 'Is it your stomach again?'

She got out the phone book, looked up a number. Dialed. 'You're seeing the doctor this very day,' she said. 'I'm too young to be a widow.'

32

Dr Ricardo, a gastroenterology specialist, asked me a lot of questions before the examination, among them if there was any case of cancer in my family. While I was speaking, he wrote down some words, fatal blood disease in the family, insomnia, indisposition, headache, nausea. He wanted to know what I ate. I gave him a more or less detailed list, explaining that ever since the nausea had started my wife had taken personal control of my diet, avoiding oil and hard-to-digest foods.

I was taken to a small adjoining room with vinyl walls and monitors. I was nauseated the entire forty-five minutes the examination lasted; I was very tense, my head throbbed. Dr Ricardo ran the flexible endoscope into my esophagus, my stomach and my duodenum, looking at the organs on the monitor screen. I was quite impressed with my insides. Even with the tube in my mouth, I tried to smile at him, as if the effort on my part could somehow ward off a tragic diagnosis. I had seen my brother die of leukemia; I knew very well what that was like. Chemotherapy and the whole shooting match. His hair falling out, that athlete, the swimmer that I had envied so much, had in six months come to look like a giant fetus in the hospital bed.

We returned to the room we were in earlier, Dr Ricardo

looking at my file, his glasses in his hand. He asked me again if I had eaten fish in the last two days. 'Did you feel anything scratching your throat?' he asked.

'At night, yes,' I said.

'At night,' he said, looking at my file again. 'At night. At night you had soup.'

'Creamed heart of palm.'

He asked me to do some further tests, blood, stools, urine, and set up an appointment for three days later.

I did everything he asked, and Melissa, more than ever, was wonderful. Without my asking, she stopped going to the country, stayed near me for everything, spoke with her friends from a laboratory, she was fantastic. Ingrid was furious. 'She does that to irritate me,' she said. 'Any woman knows that. The only thing worse than an unpleasant, fat, disagreeable ex-wife is an ex-wife who's friendly, understanding, and pretty. It's her revenge. I stole her husband? Very well, then put up with my kindness. Put up with him saying she's a fantastic girl. A companion. She's doing that out of spite, that Lucrezia.'

Ingrid didn't understand why I hadn't moved out yet, why I had to stay with Melissa until the inquiry into Ronald's death was closed. 'What's one thing got to do with the other?' she asked. 'Are you fast-talking me? Are you having sex with that woman? Is that what it is? Do you want a reconciliation? Tell me.'

Those were difficult days. I went back to Dr Ricardo on the appointed day. He analyzed the test results – blood, urine, everything normal. The endoscopy had found a tear in my esophagus, a small cut, with no bleeding. I didn't have ulcers or gastritis. I had probably ingested some foreign body, a splinter, a small bone fragment, that caused the lesion and had already been expelled. In a day or two the whole thing should disappear. As for the indisposition and nausea, all indications were that it was a matter of stress. 'Why don't you take a few days off?'

33

From: Laércio To: Ingrid
You fabulous blonde, here's the final version of the first clause. See if it's OK for you two now.

Modification of partnership agreement – Universalis Publishing
First Clause. Item One. José Guber, Brazilian, married, writer, Identity Card #14 654 652 and Census Registry #235 765 438–53, residing at 3 Monte Claro St., is hereby made a partner of Universalis Publishing. He affirms that he has not participated in any crimes stipulated by law which might prevent his exercising his duties.

Item Two. In keeping with the above modification, the second paragraph of the partnership contract is amended as follows:

Partners	Percentage of Profits
Laércio Ferreira	80 per cent
José Guber	20 per cent

Ingrid took care of the reservations at a hotel in Malibu. The farewell scene with Melissa broke my heart. She was in the television room, in a nightgown, sad after having packed my suitcase with all good will. 'Can I give you a kiss?' she asked before I left. She was having a soft drink and I could feel her cold lips against my cheek. She smoothed my hair, affectionately, and told me to relax, she would take care of everything at our house.

My recovery was rapid. Ingrid was more and more voluptuous; we almost didn't leave the room, spending the whole day in bed. 'Sex is good for the health,' Ingrid said, 'that's why you're getting better.' Sometimes we would stroll in the afternoon around Santa Monica, Los Angeles, or Venice Beach. Ingrid loved shopping in Beverly Hills, on Rodeo Drive, and she made me spend a small fortune in those stores. In ten days the pains had gone away, I gained weight, and my disposition was vastly improved.

My negotiations with Laércio were well advanced and I was already writing my book on mysticism, which blended Candomblé, Catholicism, Hinduism, and spiritualism. Laércio had changed like night and day. He spoke of a massive campaign with billboards and posters with my picture, displays, gifts. 'We're going to make it big,' he said. He did research and laid out plans for the future and telephoned me almost daily. 'I suffered like the devil to start this business,' he told me before the trip. 'In this country, things work this way. Starting a serious business is hell, but starting a church is the easiest thing in the world. You go to the civil registry and say, "I'm a bishop and I want to start a church." They don't even ask for your ID. You say you're a bishop and bang, you're a bishop, even if you're a total illiterate. You're out of the registry office in less than five minutes with everything taken care of. And you pay no taxes, because even though those bishops have money out the ass, a church is a not-for-profit organization. Here's my proposal: we launch the book, you become a bishop and we open a church. Just look at these articles. Take them on the trip and read them. Penitents of the Purple Star. Leaves from Heaven. Blue Angels. It's the future, you understand? It's Jesus. The tithe. You gave me this insight. One goddamn good business. Jesus is the way. Jesus isn't a trademark, it's in the public domain, nobody owns it, anybody can get a piece of it. And we keep the publishing house, you go on writing your books. Except that instead of signing them José Guber, you'll be Bishop José Guber. What do you think?'

'Do bishops fuck?' Ingrid asked when I spoke to her about Laércio's plans. 'If they fuck, what's the problem? But I disagree with the church, with the word *church*. Church is for the meek poor and for resigned old people. We have to create something else, something old that seems new. That's what people like. Something new that no one's familiar with even though it's existed for four thousand years. Crystals, tea leaves, tarot cards, Chinese horoscopes, Aztecs, Egyptians, Scientology, runes, numerology, divination in general, the I Ching, the Gitas of ancient India, those things that people think have disappeared but continue to be consumed with new trappings. The idiots have a mad appetite, an incredible voracity, so we're going to feed that gaggle, we're going to make money at the expense of the credulity of suckers. Did you see yesterday, when we were on Rodeo Drive, did you see that cabala center with all those limousines at the door? The rich and famous of Hollywood only want to hear about the cabala, and the Maharesh, Maharish Rash, whatever his name is, that fat guru who preached purity and was secretly screwing the girls?'

The night I was returning from Malibu, my lawyer phoned me with the news I'd been waiting for so long. Ronald's case was closed. The matter was filed away.

'Now,' Ingrid said, 'you don't have any excuse. Enough of Lucrezia Borgia. What is it? What's with that hangdog look? Do you feel sorry for Lucrezia? She's had her turn, now it's mine,' Ingrid said. 'Now I'm queen of the hill.'

'King, Ingrid, king of the hill,' I said.

34

Peaceful Refuge. Wednesday.
My thankless child, I forgive you for having abandoned your mother, because I have Jesus in my heart. It is in His name that I write; I have a message for you. Come. God wishes to speak to you. I love you. I love the lame. The infirm. The blind. The poor, like Jesus in the Bible. Life is swift, let us move with speed. Great is our God who will live on His throne until the end of time. My son, do not falter. I have horrible nightmares. I see you being devoured by the serpents of hell. From your mother, God's servant, Rosário.

The week after my return from Malibu, the stomach pains and the nausea came back. Melissa, who was already preparing for her move to the country, postponed her plans in order to take care of me, saying she couldn't leave me in that condition.

I did a laparoscopy, colonoscopy, CAT scan, magnetic resonance imaging, abdominal ultrasonography, and a complete examination of the digestive tract. The doctors were unable to diagnose my problem. They suspected some kind of rare disease brought on by the pigeons of southern California.

On one of my visits to the clinic, I saw in the waiting room a pale young girl accompanied by an older woman, probably her mother. The girl's eyes were shut, her head resting against the wall, and the woman was saying, 'You'll be able to stand it, I'm here with you.' Tears streamed down the girl's cheeks. I left the doctor's office, headed down Raposo Tavares and straight to Peaceful Refuge.

I found my mother in the clinic's garden, taking care of a flowerbed, in her white gown. She was much fatter than the last time I'd seen her. She hugged me, happy and excited. We hadn't seen each other for eight months, but she didn't ask any questions, didn't throw it up to me, said only that she wasn't exactly the one who had God's message for me. I didn't even know what she was talking about. 'My letter,' she said, 'didn't you get my last letter?' I vaguely recalled it. My mother spoke to me of a great friend of Jesus, Manoel. She whistled and seconds later a fat bald man joined us, saying that Jesus had sent me a message and the message was as follows: black fruits.

'What does that mean?' I asked.

'Jesus speaks in code,' Manoel explained. He didn't know the meaning; I would have to discover it for myself. My mother related that Manoel had also brought messages for other people, that he was a messenger of God, and that I should try to make sense of those words.

'It's a warning,' she said.

Peaceful Refuge was a quiet place with a large old house, the main building, an enormous garden, various apartments, a pool, a sauna, and all the other comforts of a five-star hotel. My mother was totally at ease; she knew all the nurses, and she was treated with affection. Manoel never left her side, and I noticed that they sometimes held hands. I spent the afternoon with her; they provided me with a bathing suit and I swam with my mother and tried to teach her to dive. That night, when I returned home, I felt a little better. I told this to Ingrid by phone and we laughed at the story of the black fruits. 'Take advantage of having your mother,' she said. 'I still miss mine even now.'

I started visiting my mother more frequently. At first, I listened perfunctorily to the stories she and Manoel would tell. Later, I began paying more attention and writing things down. That gave me peace. Besides which, it was providing me with some good material for the book.

'You don't believe the crazy things your mother says, do you?' Ingrid asked. 'It's one thing to write those books, I saw God, God told me, "I love you," black fruits, that's one thing, and it's something else entirely to believe all that twaddle.'

I really tried not to believe. But it's hard not to believe in God with this pain in my stomach.

35

Guber, take a look at the design for the billboards.
Cordially, Laércio.

Billboard #1 – First Phase
A white background, red letters: Discover the real name of João Aroeira.
Watch for: *Conversations with the Creator.*

Billboard #2 – Prelaunch Phase
A photo of José Guber, all in white, blue background.
Slogan: José Guber, the real name of João Aroeira.

Billboard #3 – Launch Phase
Cover of the book *Conversations with the Creator,* by José Guber. Photo of the author, in a white suit, the kind for a romantic singer's album cover.
Slogan: *Give Yourself a Hand*: buy José Guber's book.

During Carnival, Ingrid and I went to Acapulco. I was putting the finishing touches on the book, vomiting non-stop; the doctor suggested I leave São Paulo, breathe clean air, swim in cold water. We rented an oceanfront cottage. At night, I would work on the book, after we returned from the casino. During the day, I was obliged to go on boat trips with a straw hat on my head, fish, walk along the beach, and spend money.

That night, I was writing, Ingrid in the bed in a nightgown, with a pen and notebook in her hand. 'Come over here,' she said, 'I want to show you something.' I lay down beside her and saw the following handwritten entries:

Wednesday the 11th – vomiting, headache, São Paulo
Thursday the 12th – vomiting, headache, São Paulo
Friday the 13th – vomiting, headache, São Paulo
Saturday the 14th – headache, Ubatuba
Sunday the 15th – slight headache, Ubatuba
Monday the 16th – no illness, Ubatuba
Tuesday the 17th – headache, São Paulo
Wednesday the 18th – vomiting, headache, São Paulo
Thursday the 19th – headache, Campinas
Friday the 20th – headache, Campinas
Saturday the 21st – nausea, headache, São Paulo
Sunday the 22nd – vomiting, drop in blood pressure, headache, São Paulo

I read Ingrid's entries. 'Since we returned from Malibu,' Ingrid said, 'I've been noticing something. You only get better when you're not at home.'

I sat down on the bed. 'Maybe the doctor's theory that I suffer from stress, a problem with an emotional basis, is correct.'

'Are you the type to have problems with an emotional basis? Look at it, you only get better when we travel.'

'That's true,' I said, looking at the list again.

'Want to know my theory?' Ingrid said. 'Melissa is poisoning you. That's why she makes such a point of taking care of you, that's why Lucrezia Borgia has been so devoted to you. Now I understand why she asked you to not make the separation official until after the investigation of Ronald's death was closed. The scheming bitch was trying to stall for time. Think about it. Now that the inquiry has been closed, why hasn't she moved to the country? Wasn't that what the two of you agreed?'

'Yes,' I said.

'Well then? Why do you look so surprised? Every woman dreams about killing her husband. If you die she's going to be very well off, the house, plus Universalis, plus all your money. Why are you resisting so hard believing that people can also have a cruel side? Aren't you sitting there, writing a book to scam dummies?'

'Hey,' I said.

'What's the matter? It's me, Ingrid. Your Ingrid. You can speak freely with me. It's nothing but a shuck, talk with God, God exercise, something-or-other mantra, we both know it's pure opportunism. Why can't Melissa do her bit of wickedness too? What's the difference between conning the husband who left her for another woman and conning stupid readers? Lucrezia isn't the person you think she is. It's all a lie. As Laércio says, I know the human soul. Nobody works with snakes, feeds snakes, tosses rats into the pit, stuffs rabbits down rattlers' mouths, by accident,' Ingrid said.

Ingrid's list intrigued me a little, but I didn't believe it. Melissa and I had a strong bond, and Ingrid didn't know that. We had killed a man; that united us. Since then, more and more, we had dedicated ourselves to each other, isolated ourselves; for some time life was only Melissa and I and nothing else, each taking care of the other. She gave me tranquility, made me write, and I did the same for her. Killing a man represented in our lives the same thing as the death of their mother for a young brother and sister. What we suffered together at the time formed a strong union between us; Ingrid didn't know that, nor could she find out. And to Melissa the idea of separation wasn't an easy one. She was suffering, I knew that. She loved me, and I didn't want to hurt her.

Later, in bed, I promised Ingrid that I wouldn't eat at my house anymore, but it was a baseless promise. I didn't believe that Melissa could be poisoning me.

36

Dear son, we loved your letter. Manoel and I are dying to see you again. We have news about Jesus. I don't even know how to speak of this news; it will be such a change in our lives. I want to meet your girlfriend Ingrid. Tell her that we received the candy, the cheese, the sneakers, and really liked them. Manoel also liked the T-shirt from Acapulco, but he would have preferred it to have sayings about Jesus. Will you buy him a shirt that says I'm a Friend of Jesus? Manoel thinks we should also speak of our love for Jesus. That is also my opinion. Manoel and I agree about everything. Did you know that he likes Brussels sprouts, just as I do? I don't know a single other person who likes Brussels sprouts. Your father liked Brussels sprouts. Now, II Chronicles: 'They mocked the messengers of God, and despised his words, and misused his prophets, until the wrath of the Lord arose against his people, till there was no remedy.'

On the day that I handed the book in to Laércio, I woke up feeling especially bad. I went to the kitchen and found an older woman, one Mercedes, in front of the stove, preparing food for freezing. She introduced herself and explained she'd been Dona Melissa's cook 'in Mr Ronald's time, poor Mr Ronald, God rest his soul.' She said that Melissa was worried about my health and had asked her to prepare some food to store in the freezer. Melissa alerted Mercedes to only use filtered water because of my problem. I asked for tea and went to sit in the garden.

The house was a mess, with Melissa's boxes everywhere; she was moving to the country that weekend.

The sky was blue, it was a pleasant day, but I couldn't stay in the sun. The nausea had increased; I had to go to my room, where I spent the morning in bed. In the afternoon, Mercedes entered my bedroom and placed on the night table a steaming pot of some foul-smelling dark liquid. She said that she used to prepare the infusion for Mr Ronald. That was news, that Ronald had suffered from his stomach like me.

'Oh really?' I asked.

'The poor man was all the time vomiting,' she said. 'Dr Cisne almost lost his mind over it. They never did find out what the illness was.'

I felt a chill that began at the base of my spine and traveled all the way to the tip of my tongue. Black fruits.

'She must be trying to poison me,' I said.

Mercedes laughed at my joke. She laughed because I must be paying her well. Deep down, she didn't find the least bit of humor in my comment.

Piles and piles of boxes scattered around Melissa's bedroom. It didn't take me long to find an old address book, one of those refillable leather ones. I went straight to the letter C. There he was, Dr Cisne, gastroenterologist, 8661–7524.

I dialed. Dr Cisne was with a patient and only answered on the third try. In my encyclopedia salesman's voice, I identified myself as Pedro, a police detective, saying that I wouldn't take up much of his time, I just had a few quick questions. Yes, Ronald was his patient. Yes, Ronald suffered from an unidentified gastric disturbance, probably the result of emotional problems. 'Why don't you come by here?' he asked. 'I can check the details in my files.' I hung up.

I was closing the address book when I noticed a piece of paper sticking out of the leather. I pulled it out. An envelope with Melissa's name. In the upper left-hand corner was a logo, a stagecoach with two cowboys in the driver's seat, one of them holding a Winchester with the barrel pointing upward. Wells Fargo Bank, PO Box 5008, Campbell CA. I opened it. Inside was a bank statement; balance three million, two hundred thousand dollars. I looked again. Three million, two hundred thousand dollars.

I took a cold shower, three million dollars, I got out, had something to eat at the corner, three million, went back and waited in the living room, waiting for Melissa to arrive, the envelope in my hand.

37

At two in the morning, a car pulled up in front of my house. Melissa jumped out quickly, came around the side of the vehicle, and said goodbye to the driver. When she saw me on the sofa with all the lights on, Melissa immediately went into her role of the concerned model ex-wife, with her usual talent. She kissed me on the brow, said she was exhausted, that she'd been all this time talking to a businessman from Diablo Valley, a specialist in Australian pythons. She asked if I was better, if I had eaten what she'd prepared, if I would like some herbal tea.

I showed her the statement from the Wells Fargo Bank.

She sat in the armchair, putting her feet on the center table, on my art books. 'It's Ronald's money,' she said casually.

I asked if it was money she had received at Ronald's death, from the insurance. 'There's no policy worth that much, and you know that very well,' she said.

'I understand, insurance and some other scams.'

She got up, went to the bar, got a bottle of whiskey, a glass with ice, and began talking about how much I'd fucked up her life. 'Don't point your finger at me,' she said, 'the betrayer here is you. No sooner were we married than you started fucking a secretary. You didn't even bother looking for something better, you grabbed the first thing within reach, a secretary,' she said. 'You don't even feel any remorse about killing Ronald.'

Of course I felt no remorse. I had no reason to feel remorse, I hadn't killed anybody. Melissa killed Ronald. The night of the crime she grabbed the revolver out of my hand, you something-or-other, she said, because I hesitated, and she killed the maid, I would never kill the maid, or kill Ronald, or kill anybody, Melissa was the one who looked upon people as if they were those mice she stuffed down snakes' throats; the fault was entirely hers and even so I felt remorse. But she didn't let me speak, she didn't want to listen to anything, the bitch. I didn't want to listen either, I wanted to speak. 'Three million dollars, I know that's also insurance money, you murderer,' I wanted to say, you psychopath, I wanted to take her by the shoulders and shake her, she was screaming, wouldn't listen to me, my money, she said, every other word she repeated my money, said that she'd never interfered in my financial life and expected me to do the same, said that with our separation she had a right to half of everything, and yet she wasn't asking for anything. 'But if I die you get it all,' I said.

She drank her whiskey, saying nothing.

'Dr Cisne,' I said.

'I don't know what you're talking about.'

I answered that I was talking about arsenic, cyanide, strychnine, nitrobenzene, botulism, herbicide, some kind of crap like that. 'That's why you were always a shitty writer,' she said. 'You can't come up with anything original. It's all B-level: B-movies, B-literature, B-man.'

'I keep wondering whether Ronald was the first,' I said.

'Maybe there are others, three maybe, three policies comes to three million dollars, doesn't it?'

'Go to hell.'

'I'm going to Ingrid's. When you move to the country I'll come back.'

She looked at me very gravely, without saying a word, when I left the house.

Ingrid opened the door, barefoot and startled. 'Are you all right?' she asked when she saw my suitcase.

I told Ingrid that I had found arsenic in Melissa's things that night. 'That bitch,' Ingrid said. 'I knew it, I knew it, I told you so.' I couldn't tell Ingrid the whole truth, about the bank account, the three million, or my conversation with the woman preparing frozen food, Dr Cisne, because all of that would force me to talk about Ronald, and Ingrid knew nothing about Ronald's death. After Ronald died, it had taken eight months before I could sleep normally and I don't know how much longer to forget the picture of him running toward the garden, his mechanical leg coming loose from his body, his terrified expression before dying; all of it was bad for me. I didn't want Ingrid to know.

She insisted we go to the police and press charges. 'This is attempted homicide,' she said, 'we'll see that Lucrezia behind bars.'

'No,' I said.

'Are you trafficking in snakes too? Are you doing something against the law?'

'Besides the books?' We laughed.

'So what's the problem? Are you hiding something from me?'

'Of course not.'

'Then give me one reason we should let that maniac run around free.'

'She's not going to do anything else,' I said. 'She's moving to the country and will leave me alone.'

'I don't believe that for a second,' Ingrid replied.

I was tired and wanted to go to sleep. I took a sleeping pill that Ingrid gave me and we lay down in each other's arms. I stuck my nose in her fragrant blonde hair and fell into a heavy sleep, not hearing the yelps of the poodle puppy upstairs, which had been crying like a condemned man since being separated from its mother.

I awoke the next morning to the sound of the doorbell. Noise coming from the shower. Ingrid was in the bathroom. I got up.

I opened the door; it was Melissa. Across her forehead was written CAUTION, NERVOUS WOMAN. She came in. 'We need to talk,' she said. CAUTION, BAD DOG. She ran her eyes over the apartment the way animals do when they're looking for food.

Ingrid appeared in the hallway, wrapped in a towel.

'Have you told your secretary how we killed Ronald? I'll bet you haven't,' Melissa said.

'Who's Ronald?' Ingrid asked, looking at me.

'Ronald is the poor devil he murdered,' Melissa replied.

Ingrid looked at me, startled. 'I told you this woman is crazy,' I said, 'let me talk to her.'

Ingrid didn't want to go, she wanted to know everything. It wasn't easy to convince her to leave me alone with Melissa.

'Listen here,' I said after Ingrid left, 'listen carefully to what I'm about to say.'

'Don't shout at me,' she said.

'I'll shout when I feel like it,' I said, throwing her on the sofa. 'Sit there and listen to what I'm about to say. I'm only going to say it once.'

I looked at her. There was a revolver in her hand, pointed at me.

'Put that piece of shit away,' I said. I jumped on her, we tumbled to the floor, the gun, I hate you, she said, we rolled over, I tried to grab the weapon, we rolled, the revolver went off.

Melissa pushed me away and got up. I saw blood on my clothes. I saw Ingrid come into the room. Melissa slapped her face. 'Shut up, you secretary, before I put a bullet in you too.' I gestured for Ingrid to keep quiet. 'Call the police,' Melissa said, putting away the revolver, 'go ahead, I want to see it, tell them I tried to kill you.'

I felt a burning in my chest; I didn't want to look. 'While you're at it,' Melissa said, 'tell them that I also traffic in snake venom. Tell them that I sell venom all over Europe, for the manufacture of drugs. Go ahead, I'm dying for you to call the police. I've been thinking about it all night.'

At the door, before leaving, she stared at me once again. 'You're as deep in shit as I am,' she said.

If Ingrid was nervous, she hid it very well. 'I'm taking you to the hospital,' she said. She got her purse, the car keys, asked if I could walk to the garage.

38

Preparing to speak with God

The exercises that create non-space and the atemporal state necessary for a chat with God are mantric and have an extractive function. They extract from our mind the perceptive and controlling ego. This leaves us free of ourselves, to receive God.

Consonantal mantra – Balancing active energy

There are two variations:

1. With *s*

   With the body in an upright position, eyes closed, fill your lungs with air, visualize the color blue, and slowly release the air as if imitating the hiss of a snake, sssssssssssssssssssss.
2. With *z*

   With the body in an upright position, eyes closed, fill your lungs with air, visualize the color blue, and slowly release the air, pronouncing the letter *z*, zzzzzzzzzzzzzzzzzzzzzzzzzz.

Vowel mantra – balancing passive energy for the five senses (sight, sound, smell, taste, and touch)

With the body in an upright position, eyes closed, fill your lungs with air, visualize the color blue, and while releasing the air pronounce the letter A. Repeat the exercise four times more, substituting the vowels E, I, O, U.

On the way to the hospital, I persuaded Ingrid to say that we were mugged at the corner of her building by a tall, husky man with his arms covered with tattoos. 'Repeat it,' I said.

'He stuck the gun in the car window,' she said, 'you tried to resist, he fired.'

'What did the man look like?'

'Tall, tattoos on his arm.'

'What color?'

'Black, really dark.'

'If he was so dark, how could he have tattoos on his arm?'

'Then he was white,' Ingrid said.

'White. Watch the light,' I said.

'White, tattoos all over his arm.'

The blood was running down my shirt, Ingrid was driving all out, taking shortcuts, driving up on the sidewalk, making illegal U-turns, and she kept telling me everything was all right, that everything would be all right, white, tattoos all over his arm.

I was seen by the physician on duty, who examined me and advised that the bullet was lodged behind my left scapula. It wasn't anything serious, but I would have to be operated on.

When I came out of the anesthesia, Ingrid was lying beside me in the bed. 'I spoke to the detective on duty,' she said, 'and everything went OK.' She asked if I was in pain. I said I wasn't. 'Do you want to rest?' she asked.

'I want to talk.'

'Keep still,' she said. 'Yes, go ahead, you can talk.'

I told her about Ronald, the accident with the snake at the

hotel, the plan for the robbery, the crime itself, the investigation, everything, in detail. I spoke for half an hour, with Ingrid listening attentively. She wanted to know whether the police had investigated the fact of Ronald losing his leg a few months before he died. 'They checked,' I told her. 'They found my name on the list of guests at the hotel. I was called in for questioning. I claimed I had met Melissa on that occasion, helping the couple to get to a first-aid station. At that time, we hadn't gone public with our relationship, nobody knew anything about us. The detective investigating the case acted like an idiot when he found out I was João Aroeira. His wife was crazy about João Aroeira. Every time I'd go to make a statement, there were four or five books on the guy's desk for me to autograph. "If my wife finds out you're not that good-looking guy on the cover," he said, "she'll die." He became my buddy, the detective. He was always asking me about the symbiotic exercises, about how I wrote, where I got my ideas, he even invited me to a cookout for New Year's. After a time, I got to know all the detectives at the precinct. The guys loved me. That's what helped us; they facilitated everything. That's the truth. I also did a few things to please. Skillfully, of course. A TV set at Christmas, a stereo, that sort of thing.'

'Those guys only mistreat the poor,' Ingrid said.

'So what? What's that got to do with what I'm talking about?'

'It has to do with the fact that if you were poor and black, the police, with or without proof, would put you in jail,' she said, 'but you're João Aroeira, and the detectives' wives and the lawyers' wives read João Aroeira, so nothing went anywhere, and Ronald is rotting under the ground while that murderer is free, trying to kill other people.'

'Would you want me to get caught?' I asked.

'Of course not,' she said.

'You can tell the truth. Now that you know everything, do you think I'm a murderer?'

'You weren't the one who pulled the trigger, you didn't kill anyone.'

'I'm an accomplice.'

'An accomplice isn't a murderer. An accomplice is an accomplice. When you got married, didn't the police suspect anything?'

'When I married Melissa, Ronald had been dead for a year. Melissa and I got married shortly before that party at Mirna's, remember, when I ran into you? It was before that party. I stuck by my statements, but as I said, the detective was my buddy. I told him that I'd seen Melissa again at her husband's funeral, that I'd learned that he had died and had gone to the funeral, the seventh-day Mass, and that six months later the thing happened. Who can stop a free man with nothing to tie him down and a lonely widow from falling in love?'

'Falling in love,' Ingrid said, 'you'd think that was love.'

'Now do you understand why I can't turn Melissa in? Because if she told all she knows, they'd reopen the investigation of Ronald's death.'

'All right, you don't have to say anything else. I understand. That lunatic has us by the short hairs.'

'Yeah,' I said. 'By the short hairs.'

'Killing a man because of that Lucrezia,' Ingrid said. 'It infuriates me to think you did that for her.'

Two days later, we returned to Ingrid's apartment. It was then that my personal hell began. First, the telephone calls. During the day, in the evening, late at night, Melissa would call at any time, cursing and threatening, saying she'd kill me, kill Ingrid, that she'd tell the police that we murdered Ronald, that she'd kill herself, I heard every type of threat. At first, I responded. Since it was just before the publication of my new book, I thought of nothing but avoiding a scandal. But there wasn't the slightest possibility of dialogue with Melissa. She would say whatever she felt like and then slam down the phone in my face. We moved to a hotel to free ourselves of the telephone calls. But Melissa found out where we were and went on bothering us.

One day, coming out of the hotel, I saw a billboard with my photo; someone had spray-painted on it JOSÉ GUBER IS A SON OF A BITCH. I'm certain it was Melissa. Ingrid became so nervous that she couldn't sleep. 'It's not fear,' she said, 'it's hate. I never thought that hating a person meant thinking about her all day.' She hated Melissa so much that she would start to tremble when we spoke of her. Melissa even assaulted Ingrid in the hotel lobby; it was horrible. On one occasion, Ingrid found a snake on the seat of her car. In short, it was a tense period, and I came to understand perfectly how some men lose their heads and strangle their ex-wives.

The only good thing was my stomach, which was now completely healed. And the launching of the book. Laércio did a sensational job of promotion; my face was all over the city. Only the book-signing night didn't go well. We were expecting two thousand people, Laércio had spent a fortune on white wine and onion paté, if a fortune can be spent on that junk.

'How many people you think are here?' I asked.

'Less than a hundred,' he said, worried. 'If it were João Aroeira, we'd fill this shithole, we'd have people hanging from the rafters, it wouldn't be a flop like this. The problem,' he said, 'is that nobody knows José Guber,' as if he were speaking about some other person and not about me.

39

Another mage
Universalis mounts a well-financed campaign to launch a new writer of esoterica
By Renata Carneiro
We've had to put up with Pedro Jequitibá and his pile of clichés about professional success. We've also put up with the neurolinguists and esoteric experts in angels, which became a veritable national plague. As if that weren't enough, Universalis is investing in a high-priced campaign and betting heavily on yet another esoteric writer. José Guber, who earlier was João Aroeira, famous for three self-help books, *Give Yourself a Hand, The Symbiotic Dictionary of Health*, and *The Symbiotic Dictionary of Professional Success*, all on this year's best-seller list, has now launched *Conversations with the Creator*, 'a practical guide to talking with God'. José Guber is not the same matinée idol who graces the covers of his previous successes. 'Understand one thing: João Aroeira and José Guber are two different people. João Aroeira is one author, José Guber is another. João Aroeira is my pseudonym, and I'm José Guber himself.' When asked what led him to use his brother's photo on the cover of his other books, he doesn't hesitate: 'There came a time when I needed to give a face to my

pseudonym. It was a spiritual necessity. I gave it the face of my deceased brother. We were very close. My brother was a practical, optimistic person who made everyone else forge ahead. He had the soul of João Aroeira. That was the reason we used his photo.' But José Guber doesn't like talking about João Aroeira. 'If you want to know about João Aroeira, call Universalis. I'm here to talk about José Guber.' Wearing a white suit and a gold band on his ring finger, and accompanied by his adviser Ingrid Weiss, José Guber received us for an interview in the lobby of the Hotel Mar Dourado. Excerpts from the interview:

CARNEIRO: Why did you go from self-help literature to esoteric literature? To make more money?

JOSÉ GUBER: Not at all. I'm not an opportunist. Last year, I had a very serious health problem. I was in the hospital, praying, when I heard a voice in my heart, a very clear voice: 'Write,' it said, 'write.' I wrote *Conversations with the Creator*. That was it. The book was my salvation.

CARNEIRO: And how did you know that the voice wanted you to write *Conversations with the Creator* and not another book by João Aroeira?

JOSÉ GUBER: I knew that the command was to write something different from what I had been writing up to then. I just knew. I have a very strong mystic side. I've been talking with God since I was little. And it was He who saved me from the illness. I have an intimate relationship with Him. He advises me, alerts me to things that are going to happen. My book, which was a divine suggestion, shows that anyone can have that relationship, that open dialogue with God. It's a matter of practice.

CARNEIRO: What are your plans for the future?

JOSÉ GUBER: I'm writing three books at the moment, all of them about meditation. Masculine meditation, feminine meditation, and the meditation of angels, which teaches children and pure-minded adolescents to meditate. The techniques of meditation vary according to our gender. *Conversations with the Creator* is an introductory book; the others will be more specific.

CARNEIRO: Does God hear our prayers?

JOSÉ GUBER: God hears me, and even more, He heeds me. It's been said that, 'If God doesn't give you what you ask for, the problem's not with God, it's with you.' You don't know how to ask correctly. I always use the example of an American theologian, whom I greatly admire. When he was asked in an interview how prayer works, he answered, 'If you want to learn to play the piano, first you practice the scales. Chopin comes later.' Praying isn't simply closing our eyes and saying, 'I want to be happy.' You have to practice. Practice and practice. That's prayer.

CARNEIRO: Do you think there's a lot of charlatanism in the esoteric-literature market?

JOSÉ GUBER: There's charlatanism in everything. In journalism, in politics, in the manufacture of ice-cream, everywhere.

'They're sons of bitches,' said Laércio, in the restaurant, dropping the newspaper on the table. 'I don't know which I hate more, journalists or doctors. Journalists, I think, no, I don't think, I'm sure, doctors at least don't do it on purpose.' Laércio attributed the low sales of my book *Conversations with the Creator* to the negative reviews in the papers. 'I'm going to have another whiskey,' he said, 'this conversation's making me nervous. Another whiskey here, please. You see?' he said, after the waiter left. 'Not even the waiter recognized you. I spent a fortune on publicity and that goddamn waiter doesn't even know who you are. I'm going to go bankrupt,' he said. 'If your book flops, I'm fucked up the ass.'

'I'm a partner,' I said. 'I'm in the same boat.'

He laughed. 'Who put up the money? Who paid the advance? Who signed over 20 per cent of the company stock? You get fucked relatively, I get fucked royally, totally. You know I wanted to go on doing João Aroeira.'

This litany was delivered daily. Every day Laércio would buttonhole me and spend two hours telling me how my book wasn't selling. 'We did a printing of four hundred thousand copies,' he said, placing his hand on his head.

'One hundred thousand copies,' I corrected. 'We told the press it was four hundred thousand, but in reality it was only one hundred thousand.'

'What's the difference? One hundred, four hundred thousand, we're in deep shit either way.' After the whiskey kicked in, things would get worse. He would become aggressive, blame me. I had to control myself not to tell him to go to hell.

That night, when I got to the hotel, Ingrid was still awake. She said she wanted to show me something. She took me to the garage. The rear end of the car I'd given her was smashed in, badly damaged.

'I was shopping at Oscar Freire,' she said, 'and when I came back it was like this. It was her, I'm sure of it. It was that bitch.'

I promised I'd get it fixed the next day and said she could use mine while hers was in the shop.

'It's not that,' she said. 'You don't understand. Screw the car, what I can't stand any more is that maniac in our lives.'

I led Ingrid to the bathroom, filled the tub with water, dumped in all the salts and foams I could find, took off her clothes and placed her in the tub, joined her, and massaged her foot, massaged her body, told jokes, but Ingrid didn't find humor in anything.

At five in the morning, I woke up and saw that Ingrid wasn't in the bed.

I found her in the other room, in bra and panties, smoking at the window. I leaned out the window beside her.

'I've hired a guy to kill Melissa,' she said.

40

'There it is,' said Ingrid, pointing to a concrete-block construction surrounded by a high wall covered with campaign posters.

'I'll wait for you here,' I said, killing the engine. Ingrid got out of the car, went into the *terreiro*, the worship site. I turned on the radio and waited. 'Killing Melissa, hiring someone to kill Melissa, do you know what's going to happen?' I had asked Ingrid shortly before, when she told me of her idiotic plan. 'We're going to end up totally fucked,' I said, 'exactly that, nothing less. This guy you say is so reliable, this former vegetable vendor of your mother's who offered to help, the guy's going to do something stupid, he's going to try to fence a shipment of stolen TV sets, or he's going to stick a knife in the belly of some homosexual or I don't know what, he's going to be arrested, they'll beat up on him at the station house, and when that happens you can be sure he's going to give you up. And because you're my girlfriend, I'm also involved in the imbroglio. All they have to do is put two and two together. The next step is to reopen the investigation into Ronald's death, and there you are, that's the frosting on the cake.' Ingrid smoked nonstop and kept blowing smoke in my face, insisting that Dadá was trustworthy. 'Would you stop smoking while you're talking to me,' I said.

'Are we going to have to put up with that woman for the rest of our lives?' she asked. I threw Ingrid's cigarette out the window. 'She calls me a tramp, she slaps my face, she attacks me, bangs up my brand-new car, my convertible that didn't even have its plates yet, she shoots you in the shoulder, and we have to put up with that? Soon I'll take a bullet and die, is that what you want? We don't get married, we don't spend that pile of money you have, and we die? Is that what you want?'

'No,' I said.

'Yes, it is. We have no choice. Either we kill that bitch, or we die, or she turns you in. The future looks black in any case, and when I'm afraid I prefer to attack.'

'No,' I said.

'You don't know Dadá. If my mother had a bit of peace before she died, it was because of him.'

'So? He may be good at voodoo, or consoling the terminally ill, but killing and getting away with it is a horse of a different color.'

Ingrid still tried to convince me; nothing would convince me. 'Put on some clothes,' I said. 'I want to talk to him right now.'

The children playing in the street came up to my car. They asked for money. I gave them the coins that were in the console.

Ingrid returned with a guy who was on the mulatto side, his hair dyed a titian hue, white clothes, bead necklaces around his neck. 'This is Dadá,' she said. I opened the door.

'Why don't we talk right here?' he said.

'Get in,' I said.

I started the car, we pulled away. I got straight to the point as I drove. I said we were canceling the job. 'We've got a problem,' he said.

'We don't have a problem. The job is canceled and that's that.'

'We can cancel it, but I'm not returning the money. I use the money to buy medicine for my people,' he said. 'The money's gone.'

'Keep the money,' I said, 'keep the medicine. I just want to make one thing very clear: the job is canceled. Do we understand each other?'

41

My dear son, I wanted to tell you this in person, but since you are busy with God's word (Manoel and I loved *Conversations with the Creator* and everyone here at Peaceful Refuge is reading your book), since you're busy, I thought it better to write. Manoel has asked me to marry him, and I have accepted. As I have said before, Manoel and I have the same ideas and tastes, and we both love Jesus, our Lord Jesus Christ. Manoel told me it was Jesus Himself who said to him: Marry Rosário. Jesus told me the same thing; Jesus appeared to me in a dream and told me: Accept my emissary. Manoel is a messenger of God, you know. Jesus wishes our union, and that being the case, so do I, because I do the Lord's will. Besides that, it is my will also, Manoel is a very good person. (Did I tell you that Manoel likes Brussels sprouts?) Isa, Manoel's daughter, is very happy. She's a lawyer and is going to find a judge; we want to have the wedding here, among our friends. We will marry and, together, preach the word of God. I was thinking that you might be able to pay for the wedding now that you're rich. I don't know if it's true, but everyone here says you're rich. I told Manoel that if you are rich you'll pay for the party. The engagement party is on Saturday. I would like a cake and hors-d'oeuvres for all our friends and the nurses.

Tell Ingrid that we loved the peanut brittle. From the mother who loves you, Rosário, servant of God, bride of Manoel.

'Look at this writer,' Laércio said, reading a newspaper clipping, 'one more darling of the media, a young guy, he's talking about his book, the topic had nothing to do with us, but that son of a bitch reporter asks: What do you think of José Guber? Answer: I think he's trash. Take a look,' Laércio said, handing me the clippings.

We were in his office at Universalis; Laércio had called me for a meeting. 'You're enemy number one of the Brazilian intelligentsia,' he said, making a point of emphasizing the *g*. 'You've been elected the symbol of crap. Want a whiskey? I'm going to have one.'

'It's 11 a.m.,' I said.

'I wake up wanting whiskey. For me, eleven is the latest. But anyway, they're calling you an opportunist, saying that you went from self-help to esoterica because you wanted to make more money, saying that your work is the most repugnant writing in our language, you're this year's scum.'

'That's enough,' I said. 'You've thoroughly depressed me.'

'You think so? Then have a seat, because here comes the news I wanted you to hear.'

Laércio paused, smiling, sipping his whiskey. 'Take a guess,' he said.

'Just say it right off.'

'We've started to sell,' he said.

'We have?'

Laércio handed me a piece of paper full of numbers. 'Look at this. See how the numbers have been growing since

Monday? Last night, Geraldo in sales phoned me and said it had been that way all afternoon, bookstores calling and ordering copies. The numbers still aren't significant, but they signal a trend; that's what matters, the trend. I've been doing this shit for twenty years, I know how these things work. We're going to hit the jackpot. We're going to sell *Conversations with the Creator* like hot cakes. Know why the reader is going after your book? The reader doesn't give a shit about the critics. This is our revenge,' he said. 'The reader pays no attention to the critics. It's not just the increase in sales that tells me so. I have more concrete data. Have you seen the letters that have been coming in? I'll read you one. Listen to this: Dear José Guber, something-something, that's not the part I'm looking for, ah, here it is, I'll read it, "After I started doing the z-mantras, I noticed hair was beginning to grow on the front of my head." Did you hear that, Guber? A bald man grew hair. You did that. The Swiss, the Germans, the Americans spend billions of dollars to discover a cure for baldness, and you come along and prove that baldness is all in the head, it's mental, it's faith. You've made a scientific discovery, Guber. I even considered calling the press; what do you think? We'll show them this letter. Those sons of bitches will just have to lump this. It's one more thing they're going to have to lump. Hair on a bald man!'

The telephone rang. It was Raimundo, the caretaker at the country house, asking about Melissa. 'I don't know anything,' I said. Raimundo said he was worried, Dona Melissa had left the house two days ago for a meeting with Uruguayan businessmen, carrying a suitcase full of refined venom, and hadn't returned. Raimundo had phoned our house in São Paulo, but the servants also knew nothing and were worried because she had said she would sleep there Monday night and hadn't shown up.

'She must be traveling,' I said. He thought that wasn't the case; she hadn't taken any luggage.

'Shouldn't we call the police?' he asked.

'No. Let's wait a little longer. Let me know if there's any news.'

'Is something going on?' Laércio asked when I hung up the phone.

'It's Melissa,' I said. 'It seems she went away without letting anyone know.'

42

'Aren't you going to cut the cake?' asked Efigênia, one of the older residents at Peaceful Refuge.

'I want everybody in the photograph,' Ingrid said. 'Squeeze together, I want Dona Rosário and Mr Manoel in the middle. Isa, stand beside your father, that's right, you too, the nurses in the rear, Efigênia, more to this side, too much, back the other way a bit, Guber, hug your mother, that's right, everybody smile now, and . . . got it.'

The photo was taken, but no one dispersed. Doctors, nurses, residents, everybody there in the clinic's garden standing around the three-story cake I had special-ordered for the party. 'Cut it now,' Efigênia said, 'cut it, Rosário.' My mother, the knife in her hand, said she hated to ruin such a pretty cake, so white, so full of delicate little flowers and the phrase THE BRIDE AND GROOM LOVE JESUS written in chocolate.

'Don't cut the words,' Manoel said, 'I'm against that.'

'Cut it – cut it – cut it,' the residents chanted, clapping their hands.

'It's a real nice cake,' Manoel said, 'not even at my first wedding, with the dear departed, God rest her soul, did I have a cake like this.'

My mother asked me to make a speech.

'Me?'

'Of course,' she replied. 'You're the son of the bride, you have to say a few words.'

'They could be about God,' Manoel suggested.

I said the things that people always say on such occasions, we're gathered on this joyful day, love, peace, health, and so forth and so on, and the effect was extraordinary; some residents even had tears in their eyes.

'Are you worried about something?' Ingrid asked as I came away from the table with a plate my mother had handed me.

'No. Want some cake?'

'No. Is it Melissa that's worrying you?'

'I'm not worried,' I said. 'She must be traveling.'

We stayed by the pool, watching my mother serve the guests. Isa, Manoel's daughter, joined us. She had been trying to get near us since the party began, but Ingrid always found some way to prevent it. She was a woman with a nice figure, elegant, I liked her. She said she had read my book and loved it. She had also read João Aroeira. 'How do you write a book?' she said. 'Do you sit down and write or do you get the ideas first and jot them down? I've always wondered about that.'

'Well, it depends on the book.'

'Your mother's calling us,' Ingrid said, pulling me by the arm.

'Is it me or is that broad coming on to you?' she said.

'It's you.'

'I don't like the woman, she's a bore. Know what the forty-year-old woman's problem is? Not being thirty. They put on all that make-up and start looking at other women's boyfriends. Stay away from her.'

'I will,' I said.

'Do you love me?'

'Very much,' I said.

'Do you like to fuck me?'

'There's nothing better in the world,' I replied.

'Know what we're going to do when we get back to the hotel?'

'Yes, I know very well what we're going to do.'

The musicians, guitar, ukulele, flute, tambourine, drum, that I had hired for the party arrived late. When they began to play, nobody wanted to dance. The residents stood around the group and looked at them as if those young men in yellow and white were from another planet. 'They're black,' my mother whispered in my ear.

'They're musicians,' said another old woman who was beside her.

Ingrid took Manoel by the hand. 'Get your mother,' she said. We started dancing, and suddenly all the residents and nurses and even the doctor on duty were around the pool, dancing.

'I wonder,' I told the doctor later, 'if it wouldn't be a good idea to put a little tranquilizer in the Coca-Cola; they're pretty excited.'

'Let them be,' he said. 'Dancing never hurt anyone.'

'But look at Dona Efigênia,' I said. 'She can't stop running around the pool.'

The party lasted another two hours.

'This was the happiest night of my life,' my mother said as we left.

When we got to the hotel, the doorman told me there was someone waiting for me in the lobby, 'that gentleman with the beard.'

'I'm going up,' Ingrid said.

When he saw me, the man got up and came towards me. 'My name is Max,' he said, 'I'm a police detective. I'd like a few words with you.'

43

Max and I went to the hotel bar. The piano player was playing bossa nova tunes when we got there. I've always felt sorry for musicians in restaurants and hotels, playing for people eating peanuts. We sat at a table next to the window that looked out onto the street.

'I have the impression I've met you,' he said.

'That's possible,' I said, 'there's a billboard with my picture right over there.' I pointed to a gigantic poster that had been installed across the street, then regretted it. The graffiti JOSÉ GUBER IS A SON OF A BITCH was still quite visible.

'Of course, sir,' he said, 'you're the writer. I didn't put the name and the face together.'

'Please,' I said, 'no "sir".'

I offered him a drink, which he didn't accept; he didn't drink on duty. A serious young man. He took a notebook from his pocket, said he was investigating the disappearance of my wife Melissa.

I said that I was worried myself but that I thought that Melissa was traveling.

'The man who works at your country place doesn't think so. He tells us you were informed.'

'I didn't think it was a case that called for the police.

Raimundo, our caretaker, acted hastily. We're separated; I think she decided to go on a trip to clear her head.'

Max asked a million questions, the last time I had seen Melissa, if I knew of any trip or commitment on my wife's part, if she was in the habit of going on trips without letting the family know, if I had tried to locate her in the last few days, and who I had called.

'Where were you on Saturday?' he asked.

'In Rio Preto,' I said. 'I was there for the launching of my book. I stayed at the Hotel Horizonte, on Quinze de Novembro Street.'

The hotel staff where Ingrid and I were staying had already told the policeman about the scandal in the lobby, Ingrid and Melissa fighting. 'It wasn't an attack,' I said, 'they were just arguing.'

'The lady, Dona Ingrid, who was assaulted was with you?'

'Exactly. She's my adviser at Universalis.'

'Do you live together?'

'She's my friend,' I said.

Max noted my irritation. He asked for the names of family members and friends of Melissa's. 'I'm her only family,' I said. 'Melissa has neither father, mother, nor brothers and sisters. There was one aunt, who died last year, before our marriage. And there's that same lady's daughter, who I haven't met. I think she lives in Goiás, but I don't have her telephone number. As for friends, you can ask at the lab at the Institute. Her girlfriends work there. Melissa is a very reserved person. She doesn't have many friends, or a social life.'

'What about the country house?' he asked.

I explained that it was Melissa who took care of it; I almost never went there. 'With the separation,' I said, 'we decided

I'd keep the house in São Paulo; Melissa preferred to stay in the country.'

'She raises animals?'

The way that Max looked at me gave me the impression that he knew something. Maybe Raimundo had already let some stupid remark slip out. 'Cows, bulls, goats,' I said, 'things like that. There's also corn, potatoes, and coffee.'

'Snakes?' he asked.

I replied that Melissa liked snakes very much; she had worked in the serpentarium at the Institute, and she had some imported specimens, but only as pets. He looked at me for a time, as if he were studying me. He paused for a long moment. I was getting used to interrogations of that sort; in Ronald's time it had been the same thing. They bluffed, pretended they had data, made faces.

'Her ex-husband died in a robbery, didn't he? I remember the case,' Max said, rising. He wrote his phone number on a paper napkin that was on the table. 'If you have any information, please get in touch with me.'

I crossed the lobby, trying to stay calm. I went up in the elevator, and as soon as I appeared in the corridor, Ingrid opened the door. 'What's going on?' she asked.

'Get your purse,' I said.

44

On one side of the shed were the women; on the other, the men. In front, on a floor of sand and dead leaves, were the mediums, among them Dadá, smoking cigars and drinking beer. 'Today it's the indigenous-peoples ritual,' Ingrid said. 'Dadá is receiving Blue Feather, see how they're dancing?'

'Is this going to take long?' I asked.

'That woman over there, the large black woman, is the owner of the *terreiro*,' Ingrid said.

'Is this going to take long?' I asked.

'It's almost over,' Ingrid said. 'Take it easy.'

We waited for another half-hour, outside, smelling the scent of rosemary and spearmint coming from the censers.

Dadá's eyes were red from drink when he came out of the temple; he wasn't happy to see us. 'Wait here,' Ingrid said. 'I'll talk to him first; when I signal, you come over.'

'Negative,' I said. 'I want to talk to that voodoo priest myself.'

'Let me see if I understand,' Dadá said after I explained the situation. 'Ingrid comes here crying, asks for help, I give my help, I give more than my help, because I've known you since you were a child, and I knew your mother, then this guy, I have no idea who he is, this white guy, who doesn't even come to the *terreiro*, shows up here, this whoever-he-is, making a scene and cancels everything. So far so good. But now you two come back, together, wanting to know if I did the job you canceled? Is that right?'

'I'm not asking whether you did the job,' I said. 'I'm saying that the woman disappeared, I'm saying that the police are going to get involved in the story. I made it very clear the other time. I said, "I don't want you to do anything," and now the woman vanishes, vanishes just like that, without a trace.'

'I don't have anything to do with that,' Dadá said, cutting me off. 'You canceled the job, it's canceled. I'll say it in plain language, tell me why would I kill a woman I don't even know, if it's possible not to kill her? Eh? Kill for no reason at all? That's not my style. Ingrid was here, crying, I only wanted to help, and now I'm sorry. You two coming here and bothering me, pretty soon I'm going to get irritated.' Dadá turned his back and started walking away. I went after him. I grabbed him by the arm. 'Hey, man,' he said, 'I don't like to be touched, take your paws off me.'

'I hope you're telling the truth,' I said. He jerked his arm away, freeing himself.

'Let's go,' Ingrid said, 'let's go.'

We went back by the highway, in silence; Ingrid turned the radio on and off several times. 'It wasn't him,' she said, 'I'm certain of it. You can rest assured, it was Melissa herself who caused all this confusion, she's got no reason to complain, she opted to traffic in snakes, sell snakes, raise snakes, to sell venom, didn't you say she sold venom to smugglers in other Latin American countries?'

'She sells to international buyers,' I said.

'But it's illegal,' she said.

'Yes, it's illegal.'

'They make all kinds of junk from the venom.'

'They make medicines,' I said. 'The pharmaceutical industry uses the venom to manufacture anesthetics and cancer-fighting drugs.'

'It's still illegal,' Ingrid said, 'and if it's illegal that's what happened; sooner or later Melissa was bound to fuck up. Either she was arrested or they did away with her; traffickers don't have a brilliant future ahead of them.'

'She's not dead. You're talking as if Melissa were dead. She's disappeared, not dead.'

'Usually when people vanish it's because they're dead. A demented rapist grabbed her in some garage. Some robber at an ATM. A trafficker she burned, you'll see.'

'That's enough, Ingrid,' I said in an irritated tone.

'I'm no hypocrite, I'm not going to say I'm rooting for her to turn up alive.'

'I don't like for you to talk that way,' I said.

'How do you want me to talk?'

It was very hot that night; I was unable to sleep. I stood at the window, shirtless, thinking, smoking, pacing back and forth. Ingrid tried to call me to bed; I told her I wasn't sleepy. 'I'm sorry,' she said. 'I said a lot of silly things in the car. I feel ashamed.'

'You're forgiven,' I replied.

'I don't want her to die, I was just angry.'

'Fine,' I said. 'I believe you.'

'I don't want her to die just because she tried to poison you, attacked me, and bashed in my car. Come to bed,' she said, 'I can't sleep without you.'

I lay down beside Ingrid and spent the rest of the night staring at the ceiling.

The next day, several papers published the news of Melissa's disappearance. One newspaper played it up: WIFE OF ESOTERIC WRITER VANISHES MYSTERIOUSLY, said the headline. 'Look at your picture,' Ingrid said, 'it's from our files at Universalis. Laércio must be distributing it.'

Laércio called me first thing in the morning. 'Do you need anything?'

'No.'

'You don't know what it's like here. Lots of people calling, lots of journalists; I even gave a couple of statements in your name.'

The week was rough. One day, at the publishing house, I opened a newspaper and saw my name, next to the following statement: 'At night, I was doing my mantric exercises, as always, and after a time, in the middle of meditation, I began to feel a tingling sensation, a shiver, a synesthetic episode. The image came into my head of someone asking for help. A little later, a policeman came to tell me of the disappearance of my ex-wife.' I called Laércio in, showed him the article. 'I didn't even talk to this newspaper,' I said. 'What's going on? What the hell kind of statement is this?'

Laércio was embarrassed. 'Well, you were very busy, so I gave a few statements in your name, that's all. I didn't think you'd mind.'

'Well, I do mind,' I said.

'You know how it is, readers are curious. You don't know how well we're selling; Melissa's kidnapping, forgive my saying so, is helping, there's no denying it. It may be coincidence, but sales have skyrocketed. I keep thinking that if the kidnappers asked for ransom, we'd really see some sales. It was just a thought, take it easy, there's no need for that recriminatory silence, they're going to find her, you can relax, they're going to find your wife.'

My house was searched by the police, as well as the house in the country. Max apprehended a large shipment of snakes. 'I did all I could to hide it,' Raimundo told me, 'but they snooped around till they found it. Nothing to worry about, sir, I didn't tell them a thing.'

'Your wife is not merely a collector,' Max said several times. 'There were numerous examples of our protected fauna at your estate. She was doing business in snakes, which is prohibited, as you know. Dealing in these animals is an unbailable crime. If you know anything, and you probably do, it's best to speak up.'

I had learned this at the time of Ronald's inquiry: the thing is to deny till death.

Sunday night, they called me from the hotel reception desk. It was Max. 'We've found a woman's body at the Billings dam,' he said. 'There are strong indications that it's your wife.'

I said I'd meet him in fifteen minutes, at the Morgue.

45

We walked down a wide corridor, Max on my right and a light-skinned young mulatto, a morgue employee, leading the way. We entered a room filled with cots; I felt ill from the smell, a mixture of alcohol and dead flesh. 'Some kids were playing soccer near the dam,' Max said, 'and saw the corpse in the woods. Her car was found on the other side of the dam, in perfect condition. She was shot twice, once in the right temple, once in the chest.'

The employee went to the refrigerator, pulled out a drawer, and uncovered the body. I recognized Melissa's dress immediately, a blue dress with white trim; I had given it to her as a gift on one of our trips. She didn't have her diamond earrings or her gold watch. 'Was it robbery?' I asked.

Max looked at me gravely. 'You know it wasn't robbery,' he said.

We left the morgue. Max said that Detective Moreira wanted to talk to me. We drove in my car to the precinct, and on the way I felt an enormous lump of anxiety forming in my chest. Melissa's blue dress, I had seen her so many times in that dress, and that had been the last time, that was exactly what I was thinking, the last time, the last day, Melissa had died without knowing it, the last day, we all die like that, the damned last day, you wake up, I thought: It's a clear day, a blue sky, wonderful, or a gray, rainy day, it doesn't matter, that's wonderful too, you can make love with the woman you love, make a child, you can write a book, plant a tree, lie in the sun, lie in the rain, but you don't do anything, you neither love, nor write, nor plant, you simply waste the day, throw it in the trash, you go to the bank, fix the faucet, talk to the accountant, get irritated because the phone's not working right, you throw the day in the trash, and at five that afternoon, bang, you die. No one warned you that it was the last day.

At the precinct they showed me various photos, asking if I recognized any of the faces. 'No one,' I said.

'Not this man?'

'I don't even know who he is,' I said.

'Goycochea, they call him Jack,' the detective said. 'We've been after him for over a year. He's one of the biggest snake-venom traffickers in South America. He supplies venom to Germany, Israel, Japan, and the United States. You're sure you've never seen this man?'

'I'm sure,' I said.

'Your employee Raimundo has seen him twice at the country house; we have his statement here.'

'I never go to the country house,' I said.

The detective told me that Goycochea met with Melissa the day she disappeared. 'An appointment book found in the house contained very clear notes: 4 p.m., Panamericana Square, Goycochea, the 20th, see?' he said. 'A guy who parks cars swears he saw a woman matching Melissa's description talking to two men. Did you know about your wife's activities?'

'No.'

'Your information can lead us to your wife's murderers,' he said.

'I don't know anything,' I said. Deny till death.

When I left, I saw Laércio talking to the journalists who were hanging around there. 'Guber,' he said. I ignored him. 'Guber,' he shouted. I got in the car and sped away.

46

I was never a great fan of ships, but after Melissa's funeral and all those depressing scenes, I thought it would be a good idea to spend a few days on a floating island, far from everything, inaccessible, without hearing about anything or anybody. Ingrid also liked the idea.

The first few days, everything was calm. Ingrid was rather quiet, with no great enthusiasm for anything, but even so, we still managed to enjoy ourselves. We went to the pool, sunbathed, I watched the women on the boat, in those dresses, with those faces, and those husbands. It was fun, and I didn't think about Melissa's death. Actually, I felt a sense of relief, and a kind of gratitude to Goycochea, the Uruguayan trafficker. How good it is, I thought, not to have killed anybody, how good it is to be free, successful, to swim, write books, sell books, make love to Ingrid, travel by ship, without guilt, only the sun, the pool, the sauna, and anodyne conversations with the rich people who surrounded me.

Everything went reasonably well until the day the captain told me, at a splendid dinner, that a shark was following our ship. The women at our table became nervous, and the men were pleased. 'A shark,' they said. 'Why don't we kill the shark?' suggested a pediatrician. When we returned to our cabin, Ingrid was upset; she paced, sat down, got up.

'I don't know to what point we can believe in coincidences,' she said, 'but do you remember Melissa's favorite story?' I didn't remember. 'It was you who told me,' she said, 'that book that ends at sea.' I still didn't remember. 'Melissa's favorite story,' she said, 'ends with the two killers in a boat and a shark's fin circling around them.'

'So what, Ingrid? What's the problem?'

'Nothing. I just thought it was odd, that shark.'

Ingrid didn't sleep that night. I woke up in the middle of the night, she was on the deck, immobile. 'See that white mass in the water?' she said. 'It's him.' And afterwards, in the days that followed, at breakfast, in the pool, in the casino, that was the sole topic; she simply couldn't stop asking the crew about the shark. Many of them didn't even know what she was talking about, but she would insist. 'There is one,' she said, 'there's a shark following this ship.'

'Stop talking about the shark,' I said. 'It's crazy, you're taking it too far. Don't you know people hate sharks?' She promised she'd stop.

And she did in fact stop, but on the other hand her melancholiness became much worse, all the time silent, at dinner, the interminable dinner dances, she wouldn't open her mouth, wouldn't eat, wouldn't dance, silent all the time; I was the same as ever, talking, tolerating the foreigners. I would ask, 'What's wrong, Ingrid?' and she would say she didn't know, her eyes damp with tears.

'Don't ask anything else, or I'm going to start crying right here in front of those American women in their long dresses.'

I've never understood why people's behavior changes when they've achieved their objectives. For an entire year I'd been hearing Ingrid saying she wanted to marry me, wanted to be my owner, wanted to tattoo my name in her groin, wanted to put a collar around my neck, and now there I was, lying on the bed, available, receptive, all that was missing was the collar, and what was she doing? Crying.

I tried, I made the effort, I would tell jokes, dance, I even bought her a jewel in the ship's jewelry store, but nothing lifted Ingrid's spirits.

On our last night aboard, I ordered a special candlelight dinner in our stateroom. I took a leisurely shower to relax; I wanted to have a decent night with Ingrid. When I came out of the bathroom, she was sitting on the bed, looking lovely in a long black dress, her arms exposed. 'You look sensational,' I said.

'This came for you,' she said, handing me a sheet of paper. It was a fax from Laércio with the latest figures on the best-sellers in Brazil. *Conversations with the Creator* in first place. Nine hundred thousand copies. Translation contracts for eighteen countries. 'That fax,' she said, 'gave me an awful feeling.'

'What kind of feeling?'

'I don't know, fear maybe.'

'Nine hundred thousand copies sold,' I said. 'Fear of what?'

'Of change,' she said.

I asked if there was something she wanted to tell me.

'No.'

'Are you sure?'

'Absolutely.'

We embraced for a time, but she wasn't there, she was only a piece of trembling flesh.

47

Laércio,
I'm back. You need to do more ocean traveling, I've never seen so many available women in Hawaiian outfits. I stopped by the office to leave you this twelve-year-old whiskey (try not to drink before noon, please). I've given up the plans for masculine meditation, feminine meditation, and the meditation of angels; I want something of greater amplitude. I've already started on the book of positive prayer, or, to be more didactic, prayer that creates an obstacle to the negative side of the human being, which is always present in the perverse imbalance of reality. That's it. Down to work. Have the sales figures come out? I'll be waiting. Cordially, Guber.

P. S. I still haven't read the material you sent us about the cult. But Ingrid has the project in hand. She'll let you know something soon.

Juan Goycochea arrested – snake-venom ring broken up, said the announcer on the newscast. 'Ingrid,' I said, 'come see this.'

We were about to go to bed. Ingrid appeared at the bathroom door, toothbrush in hand. 'Come over here,' I said. 'They caught Melissa's killers.'

Ingrid sat beside me in front of the television. 'Goycochea is the fat one,' I said. 'I remember him, he was at our house several times. Melissa used to call him Tran-quilo because he always said that to work with snakes you had to be "tranquilo". Son of a bitch, to kill a woman that way, in a trap. It was a trap,' I said. 'Listen to what they're saying, arrested with fifty *jararacas*, you can bet they were Melissa's serpents, she had a lot of *jararacas*. What about the suitcase of venom? They don't mention the venom, and Raimundo told me that when Melissa left the house she was carrying a lot of venom.'

The commercials came on. I got up, turned off the TV. 'Very good,' I said, 'shall we have some wine?' Ingrid didn't answer.

'Look, there's something I have to tell you,' she said. But she hesitated, didn't speak. She gnawed her fingernail, paced around the room. 'It wasn't Goycochea who killed Melissa,' she said finally, standing in front of me, the toothbrush still in her hand. 'It was me,' she said. 'I had Melissa killed.'

I opened the window; the sound of cars flooded our bedroom. I closed the window.

'There wasn't time to call off the plan,' Ingrid continued. 'Dadá, from the *terreiro*, Dadá had already hired a killer, I don't know who it was, the guy was too fast. I didn't have the courage to tell you.'

Ingrid went to the closet and returned with Melissa's suitcase. She opened it; there was a large quantity of venom inside. 'Dadá gave it to me,' she said. 'By my calculations we have eight hundred thousand dollars' worth of venom.'

We stood there looking at the small vials. I felt the urge to throw it all in the garbage.

'I thought that with you at my side,' Ingrid said, 'I would

forget, but it's like a sagging breast; you look at it in the mirror and it exists, and when you put on clothes you hide it but you know it's there, and it sags, and time won't bring it back up and you can't get it out of your head. Hold me,' she said.

'Ingrid,' I said, 'everything's all right, the matter's closed, you're going to forget all that, I'll teach you to forget. I'll teach you positive prayer to block out the perverse imbalance of reality. Come over here, close to me. Give me that toothbrush,' I said. I made Ingrid repeat my prayers, and then I asked what she was feeling.

'Something is forming inside of me, a foam, a white mass,' she said. 'I think I can have that wine now.'

We leaned on the windowsill, drinking and looking out at the night. There was a party in the penthouse across the way, a floor below. People were dancing, drinking, and a redheaded woman in a red lamé dress waved at us, inviting us to the party. Ingrid suggested we go and dance a bit.

And then we started forgetting everything. I mean, more or less. Almost everything.

A NOTE ON THE AUTHOR AND TRANSLATOR

Patrícia Melo is a young screenwriter, playwright as well as novelist. She lives in São Paulo.

Clifford E. Landers is Professor of Political Science in New Jersey City University. His translations from Brazilian Portuguese include novels by Rubem Fonseca, Jorge Amado, João Ubaldo Ribeiro, Patrícia Melo, Chico Buarque, Jô Soares, Paulo Coelho, Marcos Rey, and José de Alencar, as well as shorter fiction by Lima Barreto, Rachel de Queiroz, and Osman Lins. He is currently translating the best-seller *Cidade de Deus*, by Paulo Lins.